Sighted

Susan Monroe McGrath

Susan Monroe McGrath

Contents

Chapter One

I killed a man on my sixteenth birthday.

I wish it weren't true, but that would mean it was all in my imagination. It would mean I don't really have visions. That I can't see disaster before it strikes. It would mean I can't change fate.

My visions have allowed me to save four lives, and prevent a handful of injuries.

Manuel Striker is my only failure. His death is the vision that haunts me. His death is the one I failed to prevent.

I killed him.

It's my secret.

I pretend the future doesn't unfold in front of me, invite me to change it. No one would believe I see what I see. They would think I've lost my mind or have an overactive imagination.

Sometimes I think that myself. Sometimes I wish that were the truth.

This morning, I am at home, walking down the stairs when a vision hits. As usual, my body stops in the midst of what I am doing while my vision flies free. Today this saves me from tumbling down the stairs.

What I see doesn't change much when the vision hits. I still see our kitchen, but my sight has zoomed in.

I am seated at the island, Nik to my left, Dad to my right. Mom is in front of me, across the island. She smiles, then turns to open the oven. Luna is on the prowl. Her nose perks at the scents in the air. Before Mom can swing the oven door closed, Luna leaps.

The vision stops as quickly as it started. I am no longer sitting at the island; I am standing in the middle of the stairs. Nikolas stands in front of me, his hand lifted as if he had been waving it in front of my face. I meet his brown eyes with my nearly identical eyes and smile.

"What?" It is best not to acknowledge anything odd has happened.

"Where were you?"

"Just thinking about something."

"Very intently, apparently." Nik pushes back the lock of heavy brown hair drifting into his eyes and stares at me, dares me to lie to him. "You okay?"

"I'm fine. Swear." It is the truth, mostly. I am fine. I just had a vision of one of our cats jumping into a hot oven. No big deal. This one should be easy to change.

Not all my visions are. I wish I could tell my family about the things I see, the opportunities I am given. They could help me. I am afraid that if they knew about my visions, they would look at me differently, treat me like something abnormal. I get that enough already. Too many curious, doubting stares. I am the one-armed girl who shoots a bow. I don't want to be the crazy one-armed girl who plays with a deadly weapon.

Secrets for survival.

"What do you think Mom made us for breakfast?" I ask. "Birthday pancakes?" I am not above using Nik's bottomless pit of a stomach to divert attention from my "episode."

"I hope so. With chocolate chips. And maybe strawberries." Nik's words move on to food, but his stare remains on my face. I am glad I am the only one with the power of sight, glad he can't see inside my brain. Contrary to popular opinion, twins don't always know what the other is thinking. "You hungry?" he asks.

"Absolutely. Race you." I take off down the stairs, dumping my backpack just inside the archway in an attempt to trip up Nik. He hurdles it, but trips over the two cats racing beside us to the kitchen. I tumble into a chair at the island as Nik catches himself on the chair next to me. He plops down with one hand already stretched for the plate of bacon.

"I totally would have won if it weren't for the cat conspiracy," Nik says around the slice of bacon he has jammed into his mouth.

"I didn't tell Hermione and Luna to trip you." I give Nik a smile almost as sweet as Mom's pancakes. "You should learn to watch where you're going. I didn't have any problems. Of course, the cats like me." I shove away Nik's hand and grab a slice of bacon for myself. I break off a small piece and dangle it beside my chair. Luna and Hermione twine through the forest of chair legs, drawn by the smell of a treat. The brush of fur against my bare legs tells me they are safely away from the oven. I just need to keep Luna here, on my side of the island.

"Good morning, birthday babies!" Mom turns from the stove and ignores the continued scuffle over the plate of bacon. "Pancakes?" She slides a heaping plate of strawberry-chip pancakes onto the island. Maybe Nik does have foresight.

"Mom. I love you. You know that, right?" Nik turns his attention from the bacon to the chocolate and strawberry heaven in front of him. He transfers a mountain of pancakes onto his plate, then pours a lake of maple syrup on top.

My stomach tips over at the thought of that pile of food shoved inside me. I watch Nik eat like this every day and don't understand. How does his body not reject his over-offering?

I reach for the syrup. Nik holds it out of my reach, swooping over his plate to drop more syrup on his pancake mountain.

The sound of the oven door opening draws my attention back to Luna. Her fur no longer teases my skin. I lean toward Nik to see around the island. All I see is the flicker of the tip of a gray tail. I hear cake pans land on the island in front of me, but my eyes don't drift from the tail.

I send my hand slipping across the island toward the plate of bacon. I hit it hard enough to launch two pieces from the plate. One lands right beside Nik's mountain, but the other flies farther, off the island, onto the floor. Luna's tail disappears as she turns at the sound and pounces on the wayward bacon. I shift my eyes back to the oven as Mom closes the door.

My lips curve in a hint of a smile. No burnt kitty paws today.

"Kass! Seriously! That's bacon abuse." Nik shoves my shoulder, pushing me firmly back into my seat before he reaches down to fight Luna for the bacon.

My secret is safe. I am merely a klutz.

"Mom, those smell amazing," I say. I nod at the two rounds of chocolate cake on the counter.

"Good morning, merry men! And ladies!" Dad swings around the corner into the kitchen, stumble-hopping over my bag. The Hawaiian shirt he has unbuttoned over a plain white T-shirt flaps as he flies in. "Merry ladies and man? You know what I mean. Happy birthday, kiddos." Dad drops a kiss onto my cheek, then one onto Nik's.

"Thanks, Dad." Nik rubs the kiss off with one hand while his other hand shoves another bite of pancake into his mouth. "You're extra cheerful this morning."

"It's not every day my kids turn seventeen. It's a big deal that you've both made it all the way to adulthood."

My eyebrow twitches at this overstatement. "We're not adults yet."

"Seventeen counts as adult. Sixteen is the threshold, right? You spend a year crossing over to the grown-up side of life. This last year before eighteen strikes is just polish to get you ready to barge out into the world on your own." Dad plops four pancakes onto his plate, then pours a lake of syrup equal to Nik's. He adds a flotilla of bacon. This is where Nik gets his eating habits. I'm not sure if it's genetic or if Nik learned by example. I'm just glad I dodged this trait.

"This looks great, Mina," Dad says. He stretches to reach Mom's cheek and places a gentle kiss there. Mom moves around the corner of the island to settle her hip against Dad's chair. His arm snakes around her waist, pulling her close.

"I don't feel like an adult," I say. "And have you looked at Nik lately?"

My parents turn to look at my brother. His cheeks are puffed, crammed full of pancake. The bulge doesn't stop him from trying to add another slice of bacon.

I snort out a laugh. "He's clearly not ready to be out in the world on his own."

"Oh, but look at how far you've come! You're not my little babies anymore." Mom blinks hard, her normally olive-toned face tinting pink as she tries to hold back tears. Our birthday is always hard for her. She gets so emotional thinking about what we've been through. I wish we could just skip our birthday, skip the memories.

"If it makes you feel better, I won't move out until I'm twenty-five," Nik offers. "You can make me breakfast every morning, take care of my laundry, give me an allowance..."

Dad shakes his head.

Mom sniffs. "That's okay. You can grow up, I guess. I have to send my babies out into the world sometime."

"Speaking of the world outside the grand Pitera house, is this week-end your competition?" Dad looks at me.

"Nope. Two weeks." I will probably answer this question at least five more times before regionals. To Dad, competition day is always looming on the horizon. He never knows when one will actually strike. The morning of regionals will come as a surprise to him, when we all load into the car and drive to Sarasota.

"Two weeks until Shannon wins and Kass comes in second. Again. Unless she comes in third this time."

"Nikolas!" Mom shoots a glare at my brother. I just give him my tongue. I am sure he wants me to win. Deep down inside. I hope. But his words are probably close to what will happen at regionals. Shannon will win. She's just better than me.

Nik retorts with his own tongue before he turns to Mom.

The man in the green hoodie replaces Nik in my sight. Hoodie Guy steps off the curb ahead of me just as a giant yellow Hummer speeds past us and turns the corner. Hoodie Guy never sees it coming, probably doesn't get a chance to feel the impact before he is thrown up into the back window of a car parked around the corner. The Hummer skids to a stop. Too late.

Back in my kitchen, air is frozen in my throat. I push on my stomach to force out the stale air and allow the draw of fresh breath. Other than the movement of air and the pounding of my heart, I am ice. This is the worst vision I've ever had. I see Hoodie Guy every morning on our walk to school. He's not a friend, I don't even know his name, but the sight of him broken, shattered, splattered, rips through me.

A wave of tears breaks my frozen limbs. I lift my napkin to wipe my face, hide my eyes. I peek over to assess the damage. Instead of the heavy stares I expect, my parents are so focused on Nik and his doubt of me that no one noticed my absence. The conversation continued, moved on, without me.

I only half-listen to the words swirling around me. Two visions in one day, and it's not even eight yet. I've never had two visions in one day. One or two a month, maybe. Today is the anniversary of my first vision. What if this is my new normal? Multiple visions every day. Multiple people demanding I save them every day. The heart that had started to settle in my chest kicks back into overdrive.

I force myself to focus on Nik's face. One vision at a time. I can do this.

I hope.

Another vision pushes the hope aside. This time all I get are colors. White background. Splash of red. Line of gold. It stays with me just long enough for my brain to filter out a few more details out of the colors. White fabric. A spreading red pool, with a golden arrow protruding from the center of the splash.

The vision leaves again before I can process. A third vision. A vague, not helpful at all, third vision.

"What time tonight?" Nik asks. "I need to tell Joel."

Life continues in my kitchen without me.

"I'll start grilling at six," Dad says. "Tell Joel if he wants any of that veggie burger crap, he needs to bring his own. It'll have to share the grill with raw hunks of beef, though. I can't guarantee they won't touch." Dad cocks one eyebrow, a grin laced with nefarious thoughts stretched across his face.

I am stuck on raw hunks of beef. Blood. That's what was in my vision. Blood spreading around an arrow wound. An arrow wound that I might have caused. Definitely an arrow wound that I need to prevent.

But who am I supposed to save?

The only clue I have is what might be a white T shirt. I probably see twenty of those on any given day.

The gold arrow is a better clue. Mine are all black. Which probably means I didn't shoot it. I so hope that's true. Most of the arrows I've ever seen have been black. There have been a few brown, white, even camo. Never gold. That is unique enough that I will notice it.

Unfortunately, I have no idea where or when to look. Who to look for.

White shirt. Red blood. Gold arrow. It sounds more like a list for an epic quest than the clues to save a life.

I look up at the people around me. Dad has on a white T-shirt. It's more than half-covered by a blue and yellow Hawaiian print, though. I will have to hope his stripe of white shirt is not the one I just saw. Mom has on a dark purple scrub top. She's safe for sure. Nik's shirt is green.

Nik's voice pulls my eyes to his face.

"I'll let him know," he says. An evil grin eerily like Dad's creeps across his face.

I have lost track of the conversation. Who is Nik letting know what?

"Is Julie coming?"

Those words are directed at me. Spoken in Mom's voice. She looks at me. I see a hint of worry crease her brow. I must not be covering the shock of triple whammy vision day very well.

"Yeah. We're stopping by the bakery to pick up cupcakes on the way." I try to force a smile. I hope it looks better than it feels on my face.

"I'm making a cake." Mom points at the pans in front of me. "Why are you getting cupcakes?"

"Linda insisted. She's my boss. I can't really tell her no. I think she's making something special, just for us." I look at Nik. "Besides, I'm sure piglet here will eat them all."

Nik grabs the loose curl hanging by my ear and gives it a tug. "Thanks for thinking of me, Kass. You know how much I love Linda's cupcakes."

"Ow!" I smack his hand away and stand up. "Are you ready to go? We do have school today, you know. Our birthday, sadly, is not a national holiday." I glance at my phone to check the time. I'm not sure if Hoodie Guy is in danger today, tomorrow, or next week. My visions never come with a time and date stamp. I need to make sure I am at that intersection every day until I save him.

And I need to watch out for every person I see in a white shirt.

And I need to find a golden arrow. I need to make sure I don't shoot one. Or let anyone else.

So much for a happy, relaxing birthday.

"Two minutes." Nik pops out of his seat and runs up the stairs.

Mom moves around the island and picks up my backpack from the kitchen floor. She holds it out for me to slip my arms through the straps. "You okay?" she asks.

"Yeah, I'm fine."

"You just seem quiet all of a sudden."

I shake my head. "Nothing's wrong, Mom. I'm good." I adjust my backpack strap and check the clock on the wall. It's time to go. I edge toward the door as I hear Nik thump down the stairs. I turn to see him step off the bottom step, his cello hoisted in the air above his head.

"Kass, let's go!" he yells as he pulls open the front door. As if I haven't been down here waiting on him.

As if I'm not painfully aware of where I need to be, who I need to save.

Chapter Two

Nik is waiting on the driveway, his cello strapped onto the kid's scooter he has modified to cart it, earbuds tucked into his ears. I can't hear what he is listening to, but I would bet my bow it involves a cello.

Sometimes Nik and I talk on our way to school. Today we walk side by side, but alone, each of us in our own thoughts. I lift my shoulders to my ears and try to shake my muscles loose. I am coiled, tight. I want to see Hoodie Guy right now. I want to know he is still okay. Today needs to be the day I stop his disaster.

There's nothing I can do to make his most important moment come faster. I have to wait.

Once we reach downtown Delphi Springs, I can hear the dull roar of the ocean. This constant murmur, broken by boats bumping against the wooden dock is the song of Delphi Springs. It can be heard from almost every spot in town. The breeze I swear never stops blows salt-laced air over my bare skin. It is almost cool enough for me to wish for my own hoodie.

The intersection where I usually see Hoodie Guy cross and then turn toward the docks is only half a block away. Where is he? I check my phone again. We aren't late. Maybe Hoodie Guy was early today. He could already be dead. I might have failed already.

I pick up my pace as I stare at the intersection. No blood stains on the concrete. No broken glass or shards of metal. I don't think it has happened yet. Maybe it won't even be today.

I hear the thump of heavy shoes pounding the sidewalk behind me. I turn my head. Hoodie Guy is running toward me, his work boots beating the pavement. He passes me, then Nik. He is almost at the intersection.

Under the sound of the ocean, I hear another roar. Deeper. Throatier. A growl. I jump forward, bumping Nik in my hurry to catch up, but I can't pause to apologize or make sure he is okay. It is suddenly all too fast. I step to the curb and grip the elbow of the young man in the green hoodie tightly in my hand.

He jerks to a stop and turns his head sharply in my direction, words of angry confusion bubbling to his lips. Before his voice can slip free, the yellow Hummer turns the corner. Its wheels skim the concrete of the curb just in front of Hoodie Guy's boots. His eyes widen, dilate. The realization of his near fate stops his breath in his chest.

I know exactly how he feels.

He finally pushes out a short "Thanks," before I step off the curb and hurry across the street. My heart is slamming against my ribs. I saved him. But it was close.

I am halfway down the next block before Nik's voice filters through the web of adrenaline. "Kass! Wait up!"

I stop and turn back. Hoodie Guy is gone. Nik is lifting his cello-scooter onto the curb on this side of the intersection. I take a deep breath and blow it out slowly to slow my racing heart. How do I explain what just happened? Nik saw the whole thing. This was not an act of subtle manipulation. This was me, pushing someone from in front of a speeding train. Or Hummer.

"What the hell was that?" Nik asks when he finally pulls up to me.

I still don't know what to say. I shrug.

"Do you know that guy? Did you just save him? Why did you take off so fast?" The questions bubble out of Nik. I don't have answers he can hear for any of them.

"It was no big deal." I push a stray curl behind my ear. Maybe I can downplay the whole thing.

Nik raises his eyebrows. Not buying it.

"Really," I say. "I just saw the Hummer going way too fast. We see Hoodie Guy almost every day. He crosses that intersection, just like we do."

"Hoodie guy?"

"He always has on the same hoodie." I turn and start walking again. Please, Nik, just drop it.

"Kass," Nik says as he moves to catch up to me yet again.

"You would have done the same thing." I don't look at my brother. I focus instead on moving one foot, then the other, closer to school and away from all of Nik's questions.

"I didn't see it coming. So, no, I wouldn't have done the same thing." Nik's choice of words startles me. Does he know about my visions? It's not possible. He must have meant it literally.

"If you didn't have music blasting in your ears, you would have. I heard the Hummer before I saw it." I venture a look at Nik out of the corner of my eye. He is still staring at me like I performed a miracle. I can't look at it that way, it's too much. "Stop it. You're looking at me like I'm crazy." This is exactly what I don't want. Why I keep my visions secret.

My phone buzzes in my back pocket. I reach to pull it free. A text from Julie. ANNOUNCEMENT IS TODAY!!!

"Crap," I say. I type back *Great, Happy bday to me.*

"What?" Nik steps closer and tries to see the words on my screen.

"Julie said the announcement is today."

"The announcement? Do you mean our birthday? They do that to everyone."

I close my eyes and sigh. "Double crap. I forgot about birthday announcements." I am ready to go back to bed. This day hasn't really started yet, but it has already been too much. "But that's not what Julie meant. She meant the announcement of the nominees for Greek goddess."

Nik laughs and points at me. "You're gonna be nominated. Again. Two announcements in one day. You'll be queen of the school. And by queen, I mean most stared at, mocked, and taunted of all the land." His laughter continues as he turns and walks the last two blocks to school. "This is going to be awesome," Nik says.

I am stuck in place on the sidewalk. I'm not ready to face what the rest of this day will bring. "This was supposed to be a great birthday," I mutter before I trudge after Nik. The only good part about the embarrassment awaiting me? It took my brother's mind off the saving of Hoodie Guy. Hopefully he forgets all about it.

Chapter Three

I push open the door of Spartan Sweets and send the string of tiny silver bells that hangs on the door tinkling. Julie grabs my arm, and we both stop and inhale the warm, sugary air. I close my eyes and let it wash over me, drown the ick of the day in vanilla scented waves.

"Oh, my god," Julie says next to me. "How does it smell so good in here every time I walk in? It smells like the sweet cart down the street from Nana's in Puerto Rico." I look over to see Julie tip her head back in ecstasy. "Why does my nose not get used to it? It makes me want to eat all the things. Which would make me gain a hundred pounds. But I neeeed it."

I roll my eyes and pull Julie through the doorway. Julie is not model-skinny, but she is fit, with curves in all the places girls should have curves. "You run like thirty miles a week. I think you can have a cupcake. Or two." I see a woman waiting behind Julie and pull her out of the way, revealing a little red-headed boy waiting beside the woman, his hand clutched in hers.

I take a second to check the shirts in the room. The little boy has on a plaid button-up, mom a swishy pink thing. Julie has the important parts covered by a tight black tank top. Linda has a white apron over a red shirt.

I'm pretty sure everyone here is safe.

"But I won't eat just one," Julie whines. "Or two. I need four. Or twelve. Hell, make it a baker's dozen." This earns a short, pointed glare from the mom, who is now at the counter. Linda stands on the other side, framed by glass cases of her confections.

I kick Julie's foot. "Watch it," I whisper. "Don't get me in trouble." The mom turns back to the counter to speak to Linda. The little boy pulls his hand free and inches away from his mom and closer to Julie and me.

"What happened to your hand? Why is it missing?" he asks.

I look down to see the little boy standing directly in front of me. He is staring at my stump. I kneel to bring my eyes to his level. He doesn't hesitate to make eye contact with me, but his eyes keep drifting to my stump. It is the only part of me he is interested in.

"Were you born like that?" he asks.

"No. I was born with two full arms, just like you."

"What happened?" As the little boy asks his questions, his mom turns from the counter, a look of horrified embarrassment on her face. This is more like what I am used to. People are curious, but too shy to ask. Instead, they stare. And whisper.

"I'm so sorry," the woman says. She tugs on the back of the little boy's shirt to pull him away from me. I don't know if she thinks I'm going to get angry at his questions or if she thinks I'm contagious.

I smile as I imagine her horror if her little boy's arm suddenly fell off, just because he asked me a question. I look up at the woman, but don't rise from my crouch on the floor. "It's okay. I don't mind. I'd rather people ask than stare or whisper behind my back." A light blush creeps onto the woman's pale, freckled face. I wonder how far she followed us down the street before we got to the bakery, how hard she stared at my stump as we walked.

I deliberately bend my elbow, almost waving the few inches of arm below it at her. I shift my attention back to the little boy. He looks at my stump and holds out one hand. "You can touch it," I say. "It doesn't hurt. It feels just like my other arm, it's just missing a few inches. And a hand." I smile at him. He smiles back.

"Where did your hand go?" he asks as he brushes his fingers over the skin of my stump.

"When I was really little, I was bitten by a snake. The doctors had to take away part of my arm because the poison from the snake hurt it too much."

The little boy's green eyes grow wide. "A snake?"

I nod. "A cottonmouth. I was lucky I only lost part of my arm. You should be careful around snakes. Just leave them alone."

He nods solemnly, taking my words and tucking them away for later.

"C'mon, Tyler, it's time to go," the woman says. She grips the little boy by the hand and moves him toward the door. She tosses an apologetic smile over her shoulder to me before leaving.

I stand and move toward the counter. Julie has somehow already found a cupcake and is licking the chocolate frosting off the top while she begs Linda not to let her have any more. Linda ignores the words she has heard before and moves around the counter to wrap her arms tightly around me. "Happy birthday, sweetheart!"

"Thanks, Linda." I lean into the pillowy warmth of her and inhale the spiced sugar cookie aroma she carries with her everywhere. She might be my boss, but this woman gives the best hugs. "We can only stay a few minutes. Mom will kill me if we're late."

"I've got your cupcakes all packed up and ready to go in the back. Wait here." Linda pushes away from me and hurries around the counter into the back of the shop.

"What do you think she made you?" Julie asks around a mouthful of chocolate cupcake.

"I thought you weren't going to eat any. Well, other than the one you're inhaling now. I'm not going to enable you by giving you my special birthday cupcakes."

"I didn't ask you to give me one of your precious cupcakes. I'm just curious what they are." Julie wipes a smear of frosting onto my nose. I wipe it off and plop the small blob of frosting into my mouth, letting the sugar and chocolate melt across my tongue.

"We both know Nik is going to eat them all, anyway," Julie says. Her eyes light up as she mentions my brother. She can't help it, she always perks up when she's near him, or just talks about him. "I doubt you'll even get one. Unless you eat it here."

"Mom made a cake, too. There's a chance the cupcakes will make it all the way back to my house after the party."

Julie raises her eyebrows. "You doubt Nik's ability to eat a couple of slices of your mom's cake and a bunch of cupcakes? Eating is like, his super-power or something."

"How is he any different than you?" I ask, pointing at the demolished cupcake remnants in Julie's hand.

"My weakness is cupcakes. Specifically, cupcakes made by Linda. Nik, on the other hand, will eat anything."

I laugh and turn to see Linda walking toward me with a massive bright yellow Spartan Sweets box held in her hands. The box seems to glow against the contrast of her white apron and dark mahogany skin. "Here you go, hon. I created a new recipe, just for you. Key lime tart cupcakes."

My mouth drops open, and I have to swallow to hold back the rush of saliva.

"I know how much you love key lime pie, Kass. Let me know what you think of these."

"Ooo, Linda, did you hear about nominations?" Julie brushes her crumbs off the counter.

Linda's eyes cut to me. "Again? Congratulations!" Linda sets the box of cupcakes on the counter and pulls me close for another hug.

"Julie was nominated, too." I half-heartedly hug Linda back. I am so not excited about the nomination. "There's no way I'll win this year." God, I hope that is true. I don't want to win again. I'd rather skip the whole thing and avoid all the attention. Julie, however, would thrive under the spotlight and totally deserves to win.

Linda squeals and grabs Julie's arm to pull her into the now awkward girly group hug. "You girls should get ready here! The parade starts right outside; it would be convenient for you. And I know there are people that would love a glimpse of the goddesses preparing for their big day."

"Great idea, Linda!" Julie jumps on the suggestion. "We can set up a little make-up station over there in front of the window." Julie points to a small table in front of the large plate glass window at the front of the store.

I follow her finger and see the window for only a second before the glint of sun on the glass is replaced by the glint of light on steel. A knife. Moving through a carrot. Slicing clean orange disks. A hand holding the knife. My mom's cat head ring glinting on the third finger. The knife slips, slides free of the carrot, takes root in a finger.

This time, I am spared the sight of blood. The vision cuts off before red begins to flow.

"We can put our togas on the in back, so we don't have to do it at home." Julie's voice snaps back into focus for me. "It'll be great!"

She is on a roll, and will keep plotting forever. I feel a twinge of guilt, but I cut her off anyway. My to-save list just got one item longer. "We need to go if we're going to make it to The Springs on time. Mom's waiting. Nik may have eaten all the dinner already."

Linda waves us toward the door. "I'll see you tomorrow. We've got a big cake to decorate."

I grab the box from the counter and herd Julie out the door. "I'll see you after practice tomorrow, Linda. Thanks again for the cupcakes."

"Don't let your brother eat all of those!"

I can't even pretend to care about that fate.

Chapter Four

We move from sugar into fire.

Julie and I get to The Springs picnic area just in time to witness the giant burst of flame Dad has conjured in the open grill.

"Uh, Mr. Pitera, I don't think it's supposed to do that." Joel offers his sage advice from his perch on a nearby picnic table. Black tee. Good. I smile and see Mom bite her lip to hold in a laugh. She is by a second table, unpacking condiments and chips and fruit from her swarm of fabric sacks. There is not a knife in sight.

"Good to know, Joel," Dad replies. "Would you like to take over?" Dad turns from the burning pyre to Joel and holds out a can of lighter fluid and a box of extra-long matches.

Joel shakes his head, which sends his long black hair swaying in front of his eyes. A flick of his head tosses the strands back out of his face.

"Dad, are you okay over there?" I ask. The fire is still growing. It threatens to leap forward and swallow Dad, Joel, and the rest of us.

"It'll be fine once the flames die down a bit." Dad steps away from the flames to give me a short hug. "Do I still have my eyebrows?"

I scan his face. Ash-brown caterpillars still crawl across his brow. Their usually straight tufts of hair are now curled at the edges. He is singed. "Mostly. They'll grow back. I think." I turn to Julie to ask her opinion, but she is gone. "Where'd Julie go?" I ask Joel. Dad returns to the grill and arms himself with a spatula and a pair of tongs. I'm not sure these are the right tools for the inferno before him.

Joel nods over his shoulder toward the path and spring behind him. "I think she went to find Nik. Again."

I purse my lips, then force out a breath between them. I so wish Julie would get over this crush. He's my brother. And there is zero chance they will ever be a thing.

"Does she really not know?" Joel asks. "Or does she seriously think she can overcome that obstacle?"

I shrug. "She has to know. Everybody knows, right? It's not like Nik hides the fact he's just not into girls."

Joel bobs his head. His hair bounces with the movement, making his blue eyes pop in and out of sight. "I think it's the cello. Girls dig musicians."

I ponder this for a moment. I've never thought of Nik's cello as a fashion accessory, or a feature to attract potential mates. In my mind, a cellist doesn't equal a rock star who draws girls in hordes. "Does the cello have the same draw as the guitar? Or drums?" I ask. Maybe I have missed some aspect of humanity. Maybe cellos are hot.

"It's the soul, Kass. He's got a musician's soul." As if those are his final words on the subject, Joel rolls back on his long spine until he is sprawled full length on the picnic table and closes his eyes. My mom is wise in her table choice. It would be hard to set things up around sprawled teenage boy. I watch him for a moment. His eyes flicker under his lids, as if he is dreaming. I want to know what he sees when he disappears into his head like this.

Something blunt and pokey at the same time jabs my lower back. I turn. Dad is wielding his tongs. The fire has dimmed. Dad points at Joel with his grilling tool. "What's he doing?"

"Being Joel, I guess."

"That he is. He is always Joel-y."

"That's not a word, Dad."

"It should be. It describes him well."

I hear Mom snort behind me. "He is Joel-y, honey," she says. "I agree with your dad. There is no other way to describe this boy."

I narrow my eyes and give Mom a mini glare. She is supposed to always take my side against the man-boys we live with. "I'm gonna go find Julie. Maybe I can save her from embarrassment." I don't need a vision to predict Julie will try, yet again, to flirt with my brother. It is a regular occurrence. Julie seems to miss the signals Nik isn't interested in her that way. To Nik, Julie is just another sister. Julie misses the distinction between friendly and flirty when it comes to Nik.

"I don't think I've ever seen her embarrassed," Dad says. "That girl has a freakish amount of confidence.

"It might just mean she hides it well, Dad. Honestly, I've never been sure if she's really that confident or just a very good actress." I make my exit, escaping down the short shrub-lined path leading to The Springs. This whole park is centered around a cold freshwater spring, a natural pool that offers a change from the heat of Florida and the salt-laced sea. I love it. And I hate it.

As I walk, I look from side to side, peering under the dense bushes. This path always makes me nervous. Every time I walk down it, I expect a flood of snakes to stream out from the greenery. They will swarm the path and my feet, then devour me whole.

Or, like every other time I've walked down this path, there will be no snakes at all. All statistics are fifty-fifty. It will happen, or it won't.

Julie's rich laugh up ahead distracts me from my snake-hunt. Her laugh breaks through the ever-constant sound of waves billowing on the nearby beach. I allow the sound to pull me away from the imaginary snakes surrounding me. Julie's laugh is far better to listen to than a snake hiss.

Just before the path opens into the clearing around The Springs, I stop and take a deep breath. I'm not sure what I'm about to see. I imagine Julie standing in front of the spring pool. In my mind, she strips down to her bathing suit and parades in front of Nik before she jumps into the water.

I blink hard, letting my eyelids scrub away the image. Once I step into the clearing, I see things aren't as bad as they might have been. Julie is fully clothed. But Nik and Julie are physically closer than is probably good for Julie's mental health.

She is perched on a large rock at the edge of the pool. Nik stands directly in front of her. His thighs brush against Julie's bare knees as he works. On her hair? My concern has dissolved into confusion.

Nik has pulled two long, branched fronds from one of the huge staghorn ferns that surround the pool. He is using the clips that hold back Julie's long dark hair to attach the fronds to her head like antlers. Julie has one hand on Nik's arm as he wrestles with the clips. Her face is lit by laughter.

"What are you doing?" I ask.

"It's my birthday," Nik answers. "We don't have party hats, so I thought I'd make Julie some antlers instead. What do you think?"

He takes a step back, giving me a clear view of his creation. Julie's body follows Nik's movement as if she is a planet pulled by gravity into his orbit.

"Are you making them for everyone?" I don't really want weird green antlers, but it is odd for Nik to single Julie out like this.

"Maybe. I hadn't really thought it through."

"You might get Dad to wear them if you use olive branches to form a sort of crown," I suggest. I look around. A forest of staghorn ferns, a variety of smaller ferns and mosses surround the mineral spring pool. Larger shrubs line the path back to the picnic area and separate the pool from the beach and ocean in the other direction. Not an olive tree in sight. No crown for Dad. "I don't see Joel going for it, though."

"It's okay if I'm the only one wearing them," Julie chimes in. "I don't mind being unique." I've never known Julie to shy away from attention, so this comment does not surprise me.

Nik gifts Julie with a smile. "That would save me a lot of work, actually."

"Good. Because I don't want to wear horns," I say. "You guys hungry? Dad might have the grill in a sort-of normal state by now."

"They're not horns, Kass," Nik says. "These are staghorn antlers. Get it straight."

"Whatever, Nik." I turn to Julie. "Food?"

"Yep." Julie steps close. "I don't look ridiculous, do I?" she asks in a quiet voice. Her hands reach up to straighten the fronds before they can tip backward.

"Only a little bit. You can pull it off, though." I slip my arm through Julie's and pull her toward the path. "If we hurry, we'll beat Nik back and get food before he ravages it all."

Julie and I move quickly down the narrow path. With our arms linked, we are able to block the width of the path and keep Nik behind us. His toes brush against my heels, pulling my shoes down, almost off my feet. Julie squeals beside me. Nik has his arms wrapped around her waist. He pries her from my grasp and deposits her to the side, darting past me and into the picnic area.

"Dad! Don't let him eat everything!" I call.

Joel rolls upright from his sprawl on the table. He sticks out one long, thin leg as Nik bolts past. Nik tries to dodge the barricade but catches on Joel's foot. Nik spins in a fast, dizzy circle and falls to the ground.

"Ladies first, dude. Ladies first." Joel stands and holds a hand out to Nik and hefts him to his feet.

"My hero," Julie murmurs beside me.

Plates are quickly piled with food. Joel appears unfazed by the proximity of animal flesh to his veggie burger.

"Are you going to tell the story again?" Dad asks Mom. "It's birthday tradition." Dad waggles his eyebrows as if the story he wants her to tell is somehow risque.

"Aw, Dad. We've heard it like, a million times." Nik looks to the sky for salvation. "Do we have to hear it again?"

I am tempted to correct him. We have heard the story exactly thirteen times. Once on each birthday starting on our third. I don't remember the early retellings, but I can imagine Mom settling two toddlers on her lap to tell them the story.

"It's an important story, Nik." Mom reaches over and pushes back Nik's dark bangs with her delicate, thin fingers. "It's your story of survival. I like to remember and celebrate it along with the miracle of your birth. Even though it is hard for me to tell, and hard for you to hear, I think it's important not to forget."

"Gather round, my children," Dad booms in his fake announcer voice. "It is time for the ritual retelling of the birthday story."

Nik rolls his eyes. "Joel and Julie don't want to hear this."

"Actually, I do," Joel says. "It's an awesome story, man."

I smile. I know it doesn't matter who does or doesn't want to hear the story. The story will be told. Today. Next year. Every year until the end of time.

"Well, shoot."

Dad is wiping at his chest with a paper napkin. He is smearing the blood everywhere. All over his white shirt.

A wave pushes through me. How did I miss this? My eyes fly around the park, looking for an archer, looking for a golden bow to match the arrow that sticks from my dad's chest.

I stand and take a step towards Dad. I didn't stop the arrow, but maybe I can still save him.

I look at the wound. It is not a wound. There is no golden arrow.

I have been fooled by a sea of ketchup.

"It happened on your second birthday," Mom begins as she blots Dad's shirt with a damp towel.

The words feel like once upon a time. Words that should ease me into the story gently. Instead, I feel my heart speed up. I know how this story ends. My blood. I force myself to sit back down.

Nik lets loose a long, exaggerated sigh. Mom ignores him. I smack his arm and send him a glare, warning him to be nice. This is important to Mom. Nik straightens up slightly in his seat.

"We were right here, at The Springs, where we always celebrate birthdays. You two were playing with your cousins. This was before they moved back to Greece. Kirsten was ten at the time, so we thought she would be able to keep an eye on you. We weren't watching as closely as we should have been." Mom exchanges a long look with Dad. Her eyes ask him once again for forgiveness for her mistake. As if what happened here were her fault. I shake my head. She should stop blaming herself. Everything turned out fine. We are all still here.

"Your dad and I were talking with your Uncle Phillip when we heard Kirsten scream. My first thought was that one of you had fallen into the water, and you were drowning." Mom's voice catches, tripped up by the tears in her throat. One of them escapes, slips out of her eye and rolls down her cheek. Dad wipes it away with his thumb and pulls her close.

"I don't think I've ever run so fast," she continues. "Sometimes I think it might have been better if you were in the water. It would have been easier to understand, to deal with, I think."

"We found you by the mineral pool surrounded by snakes. Surrounded isn't the right word, though. Entwined. That's better. A dozen or more thick, coiled cottonmouths were entangled with the two of you, as if you were part of one big nest." Mom stops talking. Several deep breaths enter and leave her as she looks at us and assures herself we are alive and well.

"I didn't know what to do." She tips her face toward Dad, places a hand on his cheek and smiles into his eyes. "But your dad did. He waded right in there, grabbing snakes and tossing them into the water, into the mineral spring. When there was only one left, he was able to reach Nik, to pull him free and hand him to me." Mom stops yet again to suck in another deep breath. "The last snake was stubborn, wrapped so tightly around you, Kass, that I didn't think we would ever get you free."

"Its head was so close to yours. Its tongue darting in and out as if it were tasting your hair, your skin." I squirm in my seat. This part of the story makes my skin crawl almost off of my body. This is also the part that always, always, makes Mom cry. Even though I am sitting right in front of her, she can see I am clearly okay, it will make her bawl. I hate to watch it.

"As soon as your dad touched the snake, it struck. You were wiggling, which might be what saved you. It missed your head; its fangs landed on your arm instead. Then it wriggled away, splashing into the water on its own, as if it were done with you."

Under the table, my right-hand grips tightly onto my thigh. I want to rub my stump; caress the part of me the snake took away. But I can't let my mom see that. It would undo her.

"You were screaming. So loud. But I think I was screaming louder." Mom stops talking and stares at me. "I thought I had lost you. How could a tiny child survive the bite of a cottonmouth?" Tears are running freely down both of her cheeks now. Five sets of eyes are fixed on her. No one dares to move, dares to offer comfort. It is clear this is a battle within her. None of us can touch it.

"Your uncle stepped in and bundled you up in his arms and ran for the car. The doctors at the hospital saved you. You lost your arm instead of your life." Mom's face twists into an awkward smile. She has won her battle again this year. She made it through the story. "A small price to pay, right?"

I smile back at her. "I don't miss it, Mom." I release my clutch on my leg and hold up my right arm to wiggle my fingers at her. "I've got the other one, so I'm good."

"Don't make light of it, Kassandra. You should value your arm and the life it represents. That's why we keep coming back here. Even though this place terrifies me, holds my worst, living, nightmare. It reminds me every year, every day, is a gift. A gift that can be taken away without a moment's notice."

"Kass, can I just say I'm so glad that snake bit you and not me?"

Five heads pivot to stare at Nik.

"What?" He looks perplexed by our response.

"You're glad your sister got bit by a snake? Really?" Dad stretches his arm across the table. He can't reach Nik, but he flicks the air as close to Nik's head as he can get. The spell Mom had put us all under finally snaps.

"If I had lost an arm, I wouldn't be able to play. Can you imagine me without my cello?"

"I figured out how to shoot a bow, Nik," I say. "You would have figured out how to play. You would have rigged up some sort of contraption that made it work."

"I'm sure you would have done it," Julie echoes beside me. She looks at Nik as if she believes he can do anything, even carry the sun across the sky on his back.

"Mmm." Nik disappears into his mind. I can almost see the contraption he is building in his head. "Doubtful," he concludes.

Chapter Five

My friends and family are slightly askew. None of us had trouble eating through and around the story of a snake stealing my arm. Mom even managed to eat around her tears.

The dinner gear is all cleaned up and packed away in Dad's car. All the bellies are full. Nik is flirting with a sugar coma. It is time to go home.

"Wanna ride?" Joel asks Julie. I catch a twitch in his cheek.

Julie diverts her gaze from Nik's sprawled carcass on the grass. She nods. "Sure." Julie leans over Nik and smooths the hair back from his forehead. "Nik, are you gonna be okay?"

The carcass groans.

"We'll load him up," Dad says. "Don't worry." Dad nudges Nik's leg with his loafer-clad foot. "Up, boy."

Another groan from the body on the ground. "You better not puke in my car," Dad adds.

"He looks like a freshly fed snake," Joel says as he moves away.

I feel a tremor run over me, but Joel is right. Nik's otherwise thin body bulges with the strain of containing the hamburgers, hot dogs, cake, and cupcakes he shoved inside.

"C'mon, Nik." Mom kneels by Nik. "Let's get you home so you can sleep it off."

"He's gonna feel great in the morning," I say. "I warned him not to eat three cupcakes after two huge pieces of your cake."

I also convinced Dad that he wanted to cut the cake instead of Mom. Safety first. But no guarantee that she won't cut her finger later.

My brother finally rises from the dead. He staggers to his feet and wanders in the general direction of Dad's car. I watch his zig-zag course. I am curious if he will bump into the car by chance, since there seems to be no pattern or direction to his movement. Mom takes his arm and steers him in the right direction, ruining my experiment.

"Good night, Nik!" Julie calls to Nik's departing corpse.

A groan of despair is the only reply.

Julie links her arm through mine to watch Nik heft his bulk into the back seat. She shakes her head and giggles as the door closes. "I gotta get home and write that paper for Mrs. Jones. I'll see you tomorrow, yeah?" This is not really a question.

"Jules! Let's go!" Joel's voice carries over the thrum of the tiny motor that powers his purple moped.

"Are you really going to ride that thing? I ask. I watch Joel maneuver the moped around Dad's car to get closer to Julie. It looks like an innocent, cute thing. It is a disaster waiting to happen.

"It's better than walking?" Julie answers.

"I'm not sure about that. Good luck, I guess." I haven't had a vision involving Joel's moped, so I think Julie has a chance of making it home. "Go write your paper."

Julie runs to Joel and slips on the neon green helmet he holds out to her. She climbs behind him and grabs the rack on the back to balance her weight. Joel hits the gas, jerking the moped into motion. Julie squeals and throws her arms around Joel's waist in a tight embrace. The right half of Joel's mouth tips into a grin.

I watch them wobble-roll out of the parking lot and onto the thankfully empty road.

"What do you think?" Mom steps to my side. "Will they make it home?" I wait to answer, still unsure. We watch the moped until we can no longer see it and the last of Julie's shrieks have faded away.

"If she doesn't text me by nine, I'll call and make sure she's alive," I say.

"You ready to go?"

I'm not. I didn't realize until she asked, but I want to stay here longer. "Is it okay if I stay and walk home later?" I look to my mom, expecting a no. This day always reminds her of our vulnerability. It makes her want to keep us close.

Mom tips her head as if she needs to look at me from a fresh angle. "Is everything okay?"

"Yeah." The standard answer pops out of me before I even think her question through. I'm still not sure why I want to be here, but I need to give her some reason. "It's just a really nice night. And it's almost October. The nights will be cold soon. Plus, I thought I should make my peace with this place." Ah, there it is. "It's important to who I am, right?"

Mom does not look convinced. She stares me down for a minute more. Then caves. "All right. Be home by ten? Or I'll send your dad looking for you. He'll probably be in his pajamas. You don't want that."

I laugh. "Nobody wants that. I'll be home by ten."

Mom wraps her arms around me and pulls me into a tight hug. I soak her up until she pulls back and kisses me on the forehead. Mom moves to Dad's side at the car. I watch them chat briefly, Dad's hand drifting to touch Mom's before they get into the car. I stand at the edge of the parking lot and watch as they pull out of the parking lot.

Mom and Dad wave. I can't see Nik. He must be draped across the back seat. Good thing I didn't want a ride, I guess. I'm not sure I could have moved his bulk.

And then I am alone. At The Springs. This is a first. I take a deep breath and deliberately blow it out. I turn to look at the path. The sun has moved far enough in the sky to turn the shadows under the shrubs dark and deep. It looks as terrifying as it is in my mind.

I will just ignore the shadows. Shadows are not snakes, right? I walk the path, keeping my eyes straight ahead, refusing to give in to the urge to peer under the shrubs. There is a lot of twitching, but I make it to the clearing and the mineral pool.

I settle onto the rock Julie perched on earlier. I slip off my shoes, pivot to face the spring, and let my feet trail in the cool, swirling water below. I close my eyes and let the quiet wash over me. It is lovely after the chaos of dinner. No more voices swirl around my head. The only sound is the gentle crashing of water on the nearby beach. I take a deep breath, smell the briny scent of salt and sea life.

"Hello, Kassandra." The voice is smooth and rich, a wave of caramel coming from behind me. My eyes fly open as I pull my feet up and out of the water and spin on the rock.

The most beautiful man I have ever seen is standing just a few feet away. He is tall, but not gangly. Muscular, but not bulky. A riot of curly blond hair brushes his brows and frames sea-green eyes. He looks like he is my age. Almost. Those eyes. Those eyes know things; they have experienced things. Things I don't even know exist. Those eyes look ancient in his otherwise young face. I let my gaze drift down over his shirtless torso and take in his cut abs before lifting my eyes back to his. I swallow hard. I am not sure if my heart is pounding out of fear or something else entirely.

The staring is now awkward. "Do I know you?" I blurt. I rise to my feet to try to gain a sense of balance. He is taller than I thought.

"Probably not," the shirtless man replies. "But I know you. I've known you almost your entire life." He smiles what I know is supposed to be a comforting smile. It sits on his face like a warm smile should, but I don't find it comforting at all. I feel as if I am staring down a hungry predator. A hungry shirtless predator. If he would just cover up some of that skin, I might be able to have a coherent thought.

He's not wearing a shirt. Not even a white T shirt. I don't have to worry about saving him.

But I might need to worry about saving someone else. He is clearly unarmed. At least right now. That might not be true tomorrow. Or the day after.

He'd look good holding a bow.

"Delphi Springs isn't that big," I say. "How is it possible you know me, but I don't know you?" I am surprised by the tone of my voice. I hear wariness, but it is mixed with a healthy dose of flirt. Flirting with this man might have nasty consequences.

He smiles. "I'll explain. I promise. Just not yet."

A secret-keeping, shirtless predator. "Just so you know, you're not doing a very good job of making me feel at ease." Again, the tone of my voice disagrees with the content of my words. This time the wariness roiling inside me is barely a hint, a whisper in the background. I can feel it there, hiding behind the tease in my voice and the smile on my lips. I shake my head, hard. It does nothing to dislodge the sight of him.

"Hmm." The man's smile is wide and welcoming. He thankfully pretends he can't hear my tone, as if he is reading my words as text on a page. "I have an idea," he says. "How about you tell me a story. Then I'll tell you one."

This is beyond what my wariness was prepared for. I straighten my spine and take a step back. "That's kind of weird." Weird sometimes leads to people being hurt. Or killed.

"Why? This is how people get to know each other, right?" he asks. "You feel at a disadvantage because I claim to know you, but you don't know me. This will even things out, yes?" The man steps toward me, then continues past to settle on the rock I abandoned. As he flows past me, his arm brushes mine. The contact of his bare skin against my stump raises goosebumps over my entire body.

I turn in place to follow him with my eyes. I don't trust him behind me. He looks innocent. So does a sleeping tiger.

"I still think it's weird," I say, "but sure, tell me a story."

The man shakes his head. "I want you to go first."

This makes me frown. I don't have a story to tell, not to this man, anyway. I open my mouth to protest, but he cuts me off.

"I want you to tell me about your sixteenth birthday."

Every molecule in the air stops moving, frozen in my chest, my throat. I am suffocating. I am the only person on the planet who knows that story. How can he even know there is a story to tell? I force myself to pull in a breath, force the molecules back into motion. The result is a short, shallow rattle. Tears begin to crawl up into my eyes. I shove them back down. I will not cry. I shake my head, one sharp jerk.

The man just smiles at me. "But Kassandra, I want to hear. It will do you good to talk about it, I think."

"There's nothing to tell." The words are clipped. They are also a lie. I convince my feet to take a step backward toward the path, away from this man.

The man tips his head, then slowly shakes it side to side. "Denial's not going to work with me, Kassandra. I know you can see things." I desperately want to look away, but I am stuck staring into his crisp green eyes. My feet stop moving despite my desire for them to run away. "I can't see what you see, though," he continues. "I'd like you to tell me about last year, your first vision."

Now my feet completely betray me. They take a step toward him. I am drawn to him. I am terrified of saying the words out loud, to anyone, ever. I am afraid of the consequences of owning what I did last year. Or didn't do, really. I speak anyway. My lips also betray me.

"I was here, at The Springs, with my family. For our birthday party, like we do every year. Just like today. I wandered off for a bit, came here, to the mineral pool. Then I kept walking. That way." My right arm drifts up, my finger pointing to a second path from the clearing pushing past a dense row of palms and shrubs. "I followed the path to the beach. I wanted to be closer to the ocean, I guess. There's this little, isolated beach over there. It always feels lonely. Neglected. I stood there, watching the waves wash up onto the sand, digging my toes into the alternating dry and wet."

I am in the past. I see every detail of that day again. It floats in the air in front of me, an overlay draped over the man on the rock. This is not a vision, this is memory.

"From the little beach you can see the docks in town. I watched a sponge boat come in, two men scurrying on the dock, washing freshly harvested sponges and laying them out to dry. Then I saw it. It looked kind of like an old home movie, the images flickering slightly."

"I didn't know what I was seeing. I didn't know I was supposed to do something about what I saw. I watched a small boat at sea. It headed for shore, a thin line of black smoke trickling up from behind the cabin. Then it pulled up to the dock. It sat there for a moment, a single man moving about on deck." I stop. My sight clears, the memory fading from view. I lock onto the eyes of the man. "I can't."

The man stands and reaches out a hand to push a stray curl behind my ear. My eyes close as his thumb trails down my cheek to my jaw, brushing the sensitive skin just below my ear. "You're almost there." His voice is a whisper. "I think there's only one last image."

I nod. I feel a single tear slip from my right eye and slide down my cheek. The man reaches out his hand and catches the tear on his thumb. I am not brave enough to look, to see what he does with the tear. He might have consumed it like I worry he wants to consume me.

"Kassandra. Please finish."

I stand still. The man's left-hand rests against my neck and jaw, as if it is holding me up. I keep my eyes tightly closed. I can't look at him while I say the rest. "The last thing I saw was an explosion. The boat. It just... blew up."

"I blinked and the image was gone. The sponge boat was still at the dock, the men on board still dealing with their load of sponges. No bits of broken boat. No fire. Nothing." I made it through. I open my eyes and stare directly into the eyes of the man in front of me. "I thought I imagined it. I didn't understand what it really was."

"What did you do?" The man moves his fingers over my skin. He leaves a trail of goosebumps in his wake.

I shiver. "Nothing. I didn't know I was supposed to do anything." It would have been nice if the vision came with a warning, or an instruction manual. I watch the man's green eyes as they move. I can feel them trailing over my skin. I should pull away from him, step back. I don't want to. He is warm.

"A minute later, I saw the little boat again. It was out in the water, moving slowly toward the dock. I watched it pull up and stop. I was so confused. I remember shaking my head, thinking it was deja vu, and I could somehow rattle myself out of it. The boat sat there. I watched the man come out of the cabin and move around on deck. I didn't think it would really explode. That kind of thing has never happened at our docks. But then it did. Manuel Striker died because I wasn't smart enough to know what I was seeing. I didn't save him."

The single tear that trailed down my cheek a minute ago is joined by a herd of its friends. The man pulls me close, tucks my head against his chest and wraps his arms around me. Everything inside of me is broken. Shards of me tumble out in sobs. The man rubs my back, his body sheltering mine, until the tears stop.

As I settle, I realize I am in the arms of a half-dressed man. His skin is smooth and warm against my cheek. Under his skin, I hear the steady thump of his heart. His smell is stronger this close, more potent. It is everything I love about the beach. Sea breezes and strong sunshine.

I keep my face pressed into this peaceful place longer than I should. I don't move away until I know he can no longer believe I am still distressed. I wipe the lingering drops from my face. I can't meet the man's eyes. I just told a stranger my deepest, darkest secret. I cried in his arms. I sniffed him. I don't even know his name.

"Do you know why you have the visions?" he asks. The million-dollar question. The question that makes me question my sanity. Where did they come from? Why me? The man's hands reach for me again.

I dodge. Without looking at his face, I answer. "No."

"The visions are my gift to you."

I stop dodging and take in a sharp draw of air. I lift my eyes to his. "What?"

"I sent you a gift on your second birthday. A gift that took time to develop, to grow, to... mature." A small, satisfied grin dances across his lips.

This makes less sense than any of the possible explanations I have come up with over the last year. "I don't understand."

"What happened on your second birthday?" He has turned into a teacher, leading me through what I already know to answer my own question. I have no idea what my second birthday has to do with this.

"I was bit by a snake. I lost my arm." I don't try to hide the frustration in my voice. I feel like I am being toyed with. "What does that have to do with the visions?"

"Back just a bit more. What happened before you were bit?"

I look around me. The clearing is the same as always and tells me nothing. "My brother and I. We were swarmed by snakes. Here." I wave at the clearing, showing him the lack of answers. My mind is still bouncing amongst the birthdays celebrated here. I can't connect any of them to the man standing in front of me. "I still don't get it." I wish he would just tell me what he means.

And then he does. "I sent the snakes. I couldn't decide if I wanted to give my gift to both of you, or just one. If only one, which one?" He tips his head and narrows his gaze at me as if he is pondering the question again. As if he might regret his choice. I am offended, even though I still haven't put together his story.

"It was a very difficult decision, the fate of the world depended on my choice, you see." A single, deep chuckle escapes the man. I flinch. He finds my curse amusing.

"In the end, your dad decided for me. He cleared the snakes away from your brother, leaving only you in their grasp for a moment."

I take two steps back. I need more distance between myself and this man. This long, convoluted story is bound to end badly for me. But I can't leave. It is my story; I need to hear it through to the end.

The man smiles at me, my discomfort. "The last snake, the one that bit you? It licked your ear before your dad grabbed it. It wouldn't have bitten you at all. Biting was not part of my command. But your dad startled it. It was afraid. So, it struck." His smile is all teeth. The predator again. "Perfectly understandable, really."

"The snake licked my ear? I still don't see the connection to my visions."

"The tongue of a snake can give the gift of foresight. If a god desires it." His face loses all glimmer of amusement.

I am here with a man who might be insane, possibly criminally. I know there is someone lurking, somewhere, with a bow and golden arrow. With this man's focus so tight on me, I feel like I am his prey. I want to turn, run far away. But I want to understand what I am running from more. So I stay. I ask the inevitable. "A god?"

The right side of the man's mouth quirks up as he nods. "Apollo. At your service." He bends and swings out his arm in mockery of a sweeping bow. His eyes do not leave my face. He looks like he truly believes everything he has said.

My feet backpedal, desperate to move away from the man. There is not enough space. There can never be enough space. A tall fern jabs into the small of my back, stopping me in my tracks.

"Gods aren't real." I force the wisp of air left in my lungs to form the words.

The man straightens from his bow and holds his arms out at his sides, as if he is inviting me to inspect him, see him. I stare. What I see is a man. He might be crazy, hopelessly broken inside. But his outside is beautiful. And boyish. And all man. A perfect man.

"I am here," he states. "I am real. I am Apollo."

Chapter Six

I have no idea how long I stand still and stare. I can't even wrap my mind around who he claims to be. Apollo? The Greek god? I have been surrounded by Greek mythology my whole life. A side effect of growing up in Delphi Springs, the "most Greek city" in the US. Self-declared, of course. I have heard the myths since I was a baby, studied them in school. It never crossed my mind that they could be reality.

"I don't know how to believe you," I manage.

"Honestly, it doesn't matter if you believe or not," he replies. "But things will be easier from here on out if you do believe me." The man steps back and settles on the rock, giving me space to process.

"Think about your mythology classes," he continues. "I know Delphi High offers many, and at least one is required for graduation." He smiles and chuckles to himself. I wonder what the joke is. "I love that this town is so obsessed with Greek culture that they teach about us in the schools. They should call it history, though, not mythology."

I have not moved. The fern is still pressed firmly into my spine. The small pain grounds me. "I took mythology two years ago."

"Do I look like Apollo?"

I humor him. I draw up every image I can of the Greek god. I compare this mental composite to the man who sits in front of me. Blond curly hair, blue-green eyes, chiseled features, muscular physique. He checks all the boxes, I suppose. I am not convinced the list of features makes him the man, though. "You do, but it doesn't prove anything. It's all sculptures and sketches. Not actual photographs." I wouldn't trust an actual photograph, either, but that's beside the point.

He considers this. "Hmmm. You're right." His eyes brighten and he smiles. Clearly, he has another idea. "What do I oversee?"

This is the world's worst pop quiz. I struggle to remember what I learned two years ago. "Archery, music, prophecy..." I trail off. I am not sure if the items I listed are correct or if I missed anything.

"Those are all correct. So, I could have given you the gift of prophecy, yes?"

Everything he is saying is logical. And completely unconvincing. There are way too many conditions and clauses. "Just because Apollo could have given me the gift of prophecy, if he was real, and I apparently was given that gift, if I'm not just crazy, still does not make you Apollo."

"You missed something on your list."

"What did I miss?"

"I am also the god of healing."

"Okay..." I stretch out the word, waiting for the point.

The man leans to the left and looks at the ground around his feet. My gaze follows his. Even his toes are beautiful. His eyes settle on a fragment of rock. He lifts it in his hand and turns it to look at all the angles. "This'll do."

His left-hand snakes out and captures my hand. He pulls me to him, turns the rock, and draws one sharp edge along the tender skin of my forearm before I can protest or pull away.

"Ow! What are you doing?" I try to pull my arm free, but his grip is strong, almost bruising my skin. I was right to be cautious. This man is dangerous. Reckless. Even without a golden arrow, he has drawn blood. I can't get free, so I look at my arm. The blood beads up before it runs to the side and spills off my arm onto the ground. "You cut me." The words slip out. They are ridiculously obvious.

"I did." He doesn't look ashamed or apologetic. He looks proud. "Would you like me to fix it for you?" he offers.

I search his face, looking for an explanation. His gaze is steady. Even. He doesn't seem to be affected at all by the flow of blood. I'm not sure if he is calm or just cold. I don't know what his game is, but I have to play along. I nod, the movement so small he probably would have missed it if he weren't watching me so intently.

He drops the rock, then places his hand flat against the crook of my elbow and brushes down my arm to my fingertips. His eyes never leave mine. He wipes away the blood as he passes, and the wound itself. My arm is intact and unmarked in the wake of his hand.

"Oh, my god," I whisper. My knees begin to buckle.

"Indeed." The man stands, grips my waist and pivots me to sit on the rock he just abandoned. "Do you believe me now?"

I look up at him, really taking him in for a moment. I can't imagine what he would stand to gain by lying and convincing me he is a god. I also can't imagine he is telling the truth, that the Greek gods really do exist. How else could he have healed me? Unless I imagined the whole thing. Maybe I am dreaming, or hallucinating.

I felt the sharp bite of the rock as it cut through my skin. It was not an illusion. I did not imagine it. The cut was real. He healed it.

"I think I might," I say. I pull my eyes away from him to look at my arm again. I halfway expect to see blood still flowing. There is no blood on my arm. But there are drops below, on the grass. This is real. As real as my visions.

"Why are you here today?" I ask. "Why find me now, tell me who you are, tell me you gave me the gift?"

Apollo's smile this time is pure predator. I feel my pulse quicken again, feel my body lift ever so slightly toward his. I try to pull away, but it is as if there is a rope connected to my core, pulling me closer to Apollo. I stand.

"It's time," he says.

I am so close to him that I can feel the gentle puff of his words on my cheek. The fine hairs lining my face stand up and send shivers racing through me.

"Time for what?" My voice is barely a whisper.

"Every gift comes with a price. Some sort of compensation. The gift I gave you is no different."

"Paying for a gift makes it not be a gift anymore, doesn't it?"

"Think of it as returning the favor. I gave you something. It's your turn to give me something." He lifts one eyebrow. The movement is so human, so flirty, not what I expect from a god.

"Do I get to choose the gift?" I'm not sure what I could possibly give him. What do you give a god?

"I have something in mind. It's really the only thing I would consider as an equal and proper gift." He lifts his hand and brushes his fingers along my cheekbone. I let my eyes drift mostly closed for a moment. His touch is divine.

"What do you have in mind?"

"You."

"What do you mean?" I am drifting at sea, floating on his scent, his touch.

"Give yourself to me, allow me to love you." His words are a whisper in my ear, his breath warm against my skin. I swear I feel the flick of his tongue against my ear lobe.

Snakes. Snakes started this. The cocoon he has woven around me shatters. My eyes pop open. I push Apollo away and dart around him. His body turns to follow me.

"You want me to have sex with you?" I'm pretty sure that's what he's asking. A god, demanding sex from a mortal for a gift given when she was a baby. I knew this was going to end badly.

"I thought I had phrased it better, but yes, that is the idea."

I can't quite believe this is happening. First, he convinces me to tell him about the moment in my life I am most ashamed of. Then he tells me he gave me the gift I both love and hate. He follows with the news that he is actually Apollo and mostly convinces me he is telling the truth by slicing open my arm and healing it. Now he wants to have sex with me?

I close my eyes. I need to not see him for a moment. I need him to disappear.

I am drawn to him. Is the pull coming from me or from him? Is he influencing my thoughts? Can he bend my desire to suit his? I have doubts. Which means it is my choice in the end, at least.

It would be so easy to give in to him. I can imagine wrapping my arms around his neck, pulling him close and kissing him. That's all I would have to do. I'm sure he would direct everything from there. I wouldn't have to make any decisions other than the decision to take the first step down the path. I wouldn't have to force fate where I wanted it to go.

Tempting.

But what about after? Would he disappear? Would he follow me home? Leave for now, but then randomly appear whenever he decides I haven't paid enough for my gift? Would he demand more? What would more be? I don't know what the fall-out would be if I give him what he wants, what I am oh, so tempted to give him. I don't know him.

I open my eyes. "No."

He takes a single step towards me. "No?"

I nod. I can't say it again. I'm afraid if I open my mouth, I will change my mind, tell him yes.

"Are you sure, Kassandra? I really do think it is a reasonable request." Apollo moves closer, close enough to twine a stray curl around his finger, close enough that every hair on my body stands, drawn to him. His lips curve into a tiny, wicked smile. "Your body tells me you want to, you are tempted."

He is right. I nod again, still unable to safely speak.

He takes a step back. His warmth goes with him. I miss it. I feel empty, cold.

He must see the change in my face. "Hmm. Change your mind?"

I swallow. With a touch of distance between us, I feel safer speaking. "No. I won't change my mind. I don't know you. I certainly don't love you."

"That's not a requirement, you know."

"It might be for me. That's something else I don't know. I don't know enough about me."

"Last chance." He watches me for a moment. Both of us expect me to cave. "You're certain of your decision?"

I take a deep breath. There might be consequences for denying a god what he has asked for. But I can't say yes. I can't say no again, either, so I just nod.

"All right, then. I withdraw my request for compensation."

I let out the breath. I told a god no and survived. He took it rather well, actually. I expected an argument, a tantrum, perhaps. Then I see he has more to say.

"I do have another request, though." Again, he steps close. So close this time that I can feel his muscular thighs brush against my slimmer ones. So close I have to brace my hand against his bare stomach to keep my balance, to keep him at any sort of distance. Every muscle in my body tightens as I wait to hear what his new demand will be. I'm not sure if it's in anticipation of his words or his possible actions.

"One kiss," he says.

This request is far more tempting, far less dangerous. A single kiss. From a Greek god. I have kissed a few guys, but I am sure this kiss would put those to shame. And it's just a kiss. He already agreed to my refusal of sex, so that's all it will be. One innocent kiss. I want to kiss him. I feel every cell in my body drawn to him, as if they want to fuse with him.

"One kiss?" I ask. It never hurts to clarify the terms of an agreement. "That's all?"

His eyes lock on mine as he nods and leans even closer. There is no room for the hand that has tried to keep us apart, so I let it slide across the ridges of his abdomen and curve around his side. He is warm silk. His muscles tense under my hand. I hear his breath hitch as my fingers trace over his skin. I can't stifle the smile. He wants this kiss just as much as I do.

Apparently, my smile is all the permission he needs. He shifts to close the sliver of distance that still separates us.

But this is my kiss. I will not be the submissive maiden, allowing this god to kiss me. So I move faster.

I push up and brush my lips against his. As soon as our lips touch, I stop breathing. He stops as well. We stand, frozen, for a long moment, overwhelmed by the power of the connection of our lips.

He is the first to move. He slides one hand behind my neck to angle my head. His other hand snakes around my waist and pulls me tight against him. He is velvet. He is sunshine. He is mist. His movements are slow and smooth but work to get us both breathing again. Our lips part as we share the same breath.

Apollo takes advantage of the opening and deepens the kiss. I have a tiny flicker of a thought that this is a bad idea. I should pull away. But the feel of him is too much for me to give up. I want to crawl inside his skin.

I want to continue kissing him until the end of time. But Apollo pulls away slightly and rests his forehead against mine as he looks into my eyes. I am lost.

"Please remember I gave you a choice," he whispers.

Still adrift, the words float over me. They make no sense. "What do you mean?"

"You might not like what I'm about to tell you. I want to remind you this was your choice."

I shift back, attempt to step away. This sounds like the start of consequences. Apollo lets me go. Apparently, he has no need to hold me now.

"What? What did you do?"

"Why do you think I did something?"

"You're a god. Or claim to be. Which means you have powers. You can make things happen."

"What do you think I did?"

"I don't know." I take a moment to assess myself. Nothing feels different. My heart still pounds in my chest, but that could be explained by the kiss, the sudden threat that followed. I shuffle through possibilities in my mind. "You wanted compensation for the gift you gave me. Did you take it back? Did you take away my visions?"

I don't know what answer I want. My visions are often unpleasant, to say the least. Sometimes they force me to think fast, figure out a sneaky way to change what is fated to happen. But they give me a chance. A chance to make the world a little better, sometimes a lot better. I'm not sure I want to give the chance up.

Apollo shakes his head. "Funny thing about a gift from a god. Once it is given, it can't be taken back. It is yours forever. There is no way to take the visions from you." His lips twist into a smile of wicked delight. "But there's nothing to stop me from giving you another 'gift.'"

"You gave me another gift." His mouth may be very good at kissing, but it is unable to speak a clear truth.

He nods and a chuckle escapes his twisted smile. "I did."

"What did you give me?"

"I gave you a curse with my kiss." Consequences spill from his lips and pile at my feet. "Since I can't take away your visions, I added a caveat. You will still see things that are fated to happen. But no one will believe you. No one will believe your warnings. Your efforts to change fate will fail."

I let this play out in my mind for a moment, then quickly talk through the outcome. "I will be able to see the future, but unable to change it. I will know bad things are going to happen and just have to watch them unfold. Like the boat. Over and over." I will fail. Every time. Mom will slice her finger. Blood will pour across a white shirt. I will watch people die. My breathing speeds up, the air moving too fast to allow oxygen to move into my blood. The world begins to spin around me.

"You should probably sit down." This time, Apollo does not offer to help me. He does not guide me to a seat. He stands back and watches as I stumble past and sink onto the rock. Sitting is not enough. My body says no more and begins to shut down, begins to slide me into unconsciousness.

As I fall away, I feel Apollo catch my body and lower it to the soft moss beside the rock. I hear his voice as I fade away, an echo that chases me. "We'll see how this plays out, my dear." I swear I feel the warm brush of his lips against my cheek before we are both gone.

Chapter Seven

Denial is a seductive force. It is more powerful than memory. Stronger than reality.

I embrace it, hold it tight when it wakes me on the ground next to The Spring. It carries me home, past Mom and Dad in the living room, up the stairs and drops me into slumber, safe in my own bed.

When I step into the shower the next morning I am still wrapped in its warmth. Until the water hits my skin. I don't know why this cracks the shell of denial. Perhaps it washes it away. But the first drops of water bring back the memory of Apollo. His salty sea smell. His radiance.

I only vaguely remember walking home. Maybe what I think I remember happening before I came home was really a dream. I didn't really meet a Greek god last night. I didn't refuse to sleep with him. I wasn't cursed by his kiss. Nothing about that is believable. It sounds like a hallucination. I can't allow myself to imagine any of it really happened. I must have fallen asleep beside the mineral pool and had a dream inspired by the touch of the sea breeze. Right?

A vision interrupts my rationalizations. This time I see myself. I am at archery practice, my bow in my right hand. Shannon is next to me, laughing. I can't hear in my visions, so I don't know what is funny.

Shannon shifts to strap her release onto her right hand. I watch myself strap my own release onto the stump of my left arm.

The laughter ends and we focus on the targets at the end of the field. I watch Shannon's hand in the release. The strap looks loose.

Shannon draws, lifts her bow to line her sight with her eyes. Her right arm draws back, but the loose strap shifts. Her left elbow overextends to compensate.

She fires.

The string of her bow carries the hard plastic nocking loop to her arm. It nestles in her flesh, drawing a pearl of blood to the skin's surface.

The sight of Shannon's blood on her arm is so similar to what I dreamed last night- my blood on my arm, released by Apollo's cut. It slams me out of the vision and back to the present. The shampoo bottle slips from my hand and crashes to a clattering halt at the bathtub drain.

My heart is bounding around my torso, my breath moving fast and hard. It is rare for me to see someone I know well in a vision. Someone I consider to be a friend. Most of my visions star people I don't know. A few have been like Hoodie Guy, someone I recognize, but haven't met.

This is too close.

The slew of visions that have pummeled me in the last two days have all been too close.

An arm injury could end the season for Shannon. At the very least, her aim would be off while she healed. At worst, she would never be able to shoot again.

Shannon is my competition. But she is also a friend. I can't let her suffer through the pain of an arm injury. The mental anguish of not being able to compete would as good as kill her. That girl is a little competitive.

I rinse off and step out into my bedroom with just a towel wrapped around me. I am replaying the vision in my mind, looking for the opportunity to change Shannon's fate. Julie's body tucked into the huge squishy chair by my bed startles me.

"Julie. Hi!" I'm not surprised to see her here, but the contrast to what I am seeing in my mind is jarring. And I remember I never texted her last night. "Crap."

"Good morning to you, too?" Julie replies. "Why the crap?"

"I just realized you never texted me last night. And I never called you to make sure you made it home with Joel. Thus, the crap."

"I made it home just fine." Julie breaks eye contact and begins rummaging in the backpack at her feet. A twinge of pink creeps onto her face.

"Why didn't you text me?" I ask.

"Why didn't you call me?" Julie straightens in her seat to stare at me.

I bite the inside of my lip. I can't tell Julie I didn't call because I was distracted by a vivid dream of kissing a Greek god. I can't tell her I don't even really remember getting home. She should have been more worried about my safety last night than I was about hers. "I guess I was just tired and forgot?"

"Yeah. Me too. Tired." Julie narrows her eyes a bit, then gives her head a tiny shake. "But we're both here, and we're both fine. Right? So, it's all good."

"Right," I answer. We both know we're lying. Neither of us is ready to fess up. We let it go. For now.

***

The morning is painfully slow, dragging behind me like a weight. I am antsy. I want to run to practice now. I need to know if today is the day Shannon will fail to tighten her strap properly. It could be any Saturday. I need to stop her injury.

There's also that other lingering vision. The bloody, punctured white shirt.

I'm also concerned about the safety of Mom's fingers.

Before we came downstairs, Julie claimed she was going to spend the morning working on homework. Apparently, the paper she was going to write last night has not been touched. The reality is Julie spent the morning sprawled on our living room couch.

Nik is practicing in the same room. Magnets, I swear. He is perched on an ottoman with his cello resting between his legs. One hand caresses the bow over the cello's strings as his other hand flickers across the strings at the head.

I watch Julie watch Nik. I agree, it's beautiful to watch him play. All the goofy, teenage boy stuff falls away. He sinks into the music, into the cello. He becomes one with his instrument. His eyes drift closed every time he starts to play, leaving him to play only by the feel of the instrument against him. I wonder what he sees, where he goes. I wonder if he has visions like I do.

After lunch, we resume our positions. Julie sprawled on the couch, me tucked into the corner her body doesn't take up, Nik back in music land. Julie's laptop is open on the floor below her as if she is actually doing her homework.

"God, I wish I was that cello," Julie sighs.

"Ew. You do know that's my brother, right?" My eyes fly to Nik, not sure what he would make of Julie's comment. He only hears his cello.

"Yes. I can't help it."

"You also know he's gay." Julie and I have this same conversation every few months.

"I know." Julie lets out an extended dramatic sigh. "A girl can wish."

I am never sure if she really loves my brother or just loves the idea of loving him. I'm not sure what she would do if he ever returned her attention. Wrap her arms around him? Run screaming from the room? Both seem equally likely.

"How about you wish from afar. I want to get to practice before one."

Julie reaches down to snap her laptop closed. "All right. I'm done with this anyway."

"I don't think you did any actual homework today."

"Not really. I meant I'm done staring at your brother. Kass, I think it's time for me to move on."

I turn to stare. I can feel my mouth drop open. "I never thought this would happen."

"C'mon, Kass. It's not that big of a deal. I never really thought we'd date or anything."

"It's still huge. I'm proud of you." And I wonder what sparked it. My mind drifts around Julie, the things she has said. She is hiding something. Something big. But I don't have time to pry it loose right now.

Julie packs up her laptop and the books she had scattered about in a show of productivity. "Would you be upset if I didn't go to practice with you? I think maybe I should go home and actually do some of this work."

It's like she flipped a switch and grew up in the last fifteen minutes. I'm not sure how to talk to this Julie. "Is everything okay?"

"Yeah. Just stuff to do, ya know?"

"Yeah. Get your homework done. I have to work after practice, anyway." I can call her later, start digging. I grab my archery bag and sling it over my shoulder. We leave without Nik opening his eyes. He will be surprised later when he returns to the real world and finds himself in the living room alone. If he remembers we were even there.

I watch Julie walk away for a moment, questions drifting through my thoughts. I push them aside and focus on the vision at hand. At least the one I think is most pressing right now. When I reach the school's football field, I immediately look for Shannon. She isn't on the field.

I turn to look at the bleachers behind me and the entrance that cuts through the middle of the stands. I lift my hand over my eyes to block the sun's glare. No Shannon. There are two people sitting in the bleachers. Both appear to be male. Neither of them wears a white shirt.

Peter is here, as usual. So weird. He is here every day it isn't raining, reading a book through whatever practice is happening on the field. I have no idea why he does this. He never watches our practice, or any other practice that I know of. Any time I look his way, his gaze is tightly focused on his book.

The second guy is closer to the railing that separates the stands from the field. I have to squint and move closer to see him through the sun's rays. The face doesn't belong here. Out of place it takes me a minute to sort out the features, put them in order. The curly blond hair and chiseled features couldn't be anyone else, though. It is the man from my dream. Apollo. If he is here, then nothing I remember from last night was a dream. It was real. He is real.

I stand frozen. I hear movement behind me, a call of hello. Coach Hamilton is here. I turn slowly. I am reluctant to let Apollo out of my sight. The words of his curse echo through me. Something else for me to fight through.

Coach is in his usual short blue running shorts and gray T-shirt. I have never seen him in anything other than this uniform. Shannon is right behind Coach. Her arm is intact, displayed by the FSU T-shirt with the sleeves cut off. Her jean shorts are so worn, they are almost white. The cuffs are rolled up to emphasize her long, dark legs. This is exactly what she had on in my vision. It will happen today. I don't dare move from Shannon's side. I can't walk to Apollo, find out what he wants, why is is here.

"Hey, girl," Shannon calls to me. "You ready for regionals?"

With the oddness of the last two days, I have lost the upcoming competition in my mind. It is buried under kisses and curses. I can't admit that to Shannon, though. Shannon lives and breathes competition. So, I smile and nod. "Sure. Are you ready?"

"Absolutely!" Shannon laughs. "I'm always ready!"

Her laugh makes me flinch. It crawls out of my vision through Shannon and latches onto me like a leech. This is too soon. While I am eager to change Shannon's fate, I'm not in a hurry to get to the moment itself.

"Ladies! Let's go!" Coach yells from the far end of the field. He has already set out the targets in a neat line across the far end of the field. "Fire when ready!"

I watch Shannon lean her bow against the ground. She stabilizes it between her knees as she straps her release onto her right hand. I can see the slight give in the strap, the tiny slip that reveals it is not tightly bound. The release shifts slightly as Shannon leans over to connect it with the nocking loop and arrow. This is the moment. It is time to change fate.

"Shannon? Is your release tight enough? It looks kind of loose."

Shannon cuts her eyes to me for just a moment, then rolls them and continues connecting her arrow. "It's fine."

I turn to glance at Apollo. He is real. Is the curse real too? I can't see his face clearly, but he seems to be watching us. For the first time in a year, I'm not sure what to do. It has always been so easy for me to shift events. Shannon is usually super careful with her equipment, checking and re-checking before she draws. Today she is in a hurry to ignore my words.

Before I can move, come up with a plan B, Shannon lifts her bow without a pause and looks through the sight as she draws back with her right hand. It is all too fast, but I can see everything coming in painful slow-motion in my mind. In reality, it is speeding at us like a freight train. I don't have time to change any of it.

As Shannon draws, she overextends her left arm to compensate for the longer draw length of her shifted release. Just like in my vision. "Firing!" Shannon calls, then immediately presses her release.

I close my eyes. I can't watch it happen a second time. I feel Apollo's gaze on my back, hot as a brand, in the short moment before Shannon yells in pain. "Ow! Shit."

I look at Shannon now that the damage is done. She has dropped her bow. Her right hand now clutches her left arm in a tight grip. Blood oozes around her fingers and drips onto the grass and bow at her feet.

"What the hell, Tucker?" Coach Hamilton yells from the fifty-yard line. "That was way wide!" He must finally realize something is wrong, because he breaks into a run, cuts diagonally across the field.

I lean my own bow against my bag and dig in the pocket to find my phone. "Should I call 911?" I ask. I'm not sure if I'm asking Shannon or Coach. I'm used to preventing disasters, not dealing with the aftermath.

No one answers me. I failed to change fate. Now it is like I'm not even here, not part of fate at all.

Tears run down Shannon's cheeks. She sucks in deep hiccupy breaths. I have never seen Shannon cry. I didn't even know she could cry until this moment. I thought she was made of steel. I dial my phone.

Before Coach makes it to Shannon's side, I am off the phone again. An ambulance is on the way. I return to observant statue mode, unable to do or say anything. I failed. I saw Shannon was going to be hurt. I didn't stop it. This is the first time I have failed to change fate since the boat exploded.

I watch Coach wrap Shannon's arm in an extra shirt from her bag, watch the ambulance pull onto the field, watch paramedics take a quick look at Shannon's arm and then steer her into the ambulance. Coach climbs in after her, taking Shannon's bag and bow with him.

Coach might have said something to me before the ambulance pulled away. He might have said nothing. I have no idea. I am lost in the loop of Shannon's bow string. I can't hear Coach. Instead, I hear the slip of the string, the slap of the nock into Shannon's flesh, over and over. I watch her skin part, blood running to fall on the ground. Over and over.

The replay finally shatters when a hand lands on my shoulder. It is warm, an extension of the body behind me. I lean into it, welcoming comfort. I want to pull it around me like a blanket. As if it heard my thoughts, the hand slides from my shoulder down my arm. It wraps around my waist and pulls me back into a strong chest.

I close my eyes and relax into him. I know who it is. I don't care. I will take what he will give. He doesn't say a word, doesn't ask for anything. He just holds me. Tears begin to slip from my eyes.

When the tears finally stop, I take a deep breath. I expect it to cleanse me, wash away what I just saw. But the air I breathe smells like him. Salt-soaked wood baked in the sun. The beach as the tide rolls in, my favorite time to be there.

I let myself relax further into him for just a moment. I want him to be what I want him to be for a little longer. I finally force myself to pull away and face him.

"What are you doing here?" I ask. "I didn't even think you were real, that last night was real. And now here you are. And Shannon is hurt. And it's my fault." My voice trembles, on the edge. I'm not sure if it's going to tumble into a scream or a sob.

"I am real. I am Apollo." He looks amused at my frustration. "I thought we established that last night."

"I woke up and thought it was a dream. Or convinced myself it was, I'm not sure. Would any sane person believe any of it was real? That you're real?"

"Are you sane?"

I open my mouth, an affirmation tripping across my tongue. I am forced to close it, bite back the answer I'm not sure of. "I don't know," I allow myself to whisper.

Apollo smiles and leans close, his mouth next to my ear. "You are sane. Everything you think happened last night really happened. I am Apollo." He pauses for a fraction of a second, lets the truth sink into me. "I gave you a gift years ago. Last night, I asked for something in return, which you declined to give." He pulls away. "So, I added to my gift." He laughs. "Yes, I think I will call it an addition. It certainly added to my entertainment."

I step forward, my right arm swinging, aiming to slap his face. He catches my hand just before it makes contact and jerks me a step closer. "You wouldn't want to make me angry, would you?" he asks.

His anger means nothing next to mine. I twist my arm in his grip, struggle to get free. He stares me down until I still, then releases me.

"Are you just here to watch and laugh? Is that what this is to you, a show?"

"I wanted to see what happened as a result of your choice. I knew it wouldn't take long for fate to catch up with you. Mortals always think they can control the gods, outwit us, turn things in their favor." He leans close again, this time letting his lips brush against my ear. "It never works that way," he whispers. The words flutter into my ear.

His breath against my skin, his warmth close enough to seep into me, his smell. They all work against me. Despite my anger that he cursed me, stopped me from helping Shannon, I still feel drawn to the jerk. The ripple of gooseflesh starts at the nape of my neck, radiating outward, raising hairs all over my body. I close my eyes. I want to shut him out and focus on the smell and feel of him at the same time.

Apollo inches closer and aligns his body with mine. His lips still hover over my ear. "You might be able to convince me to turn things in your favor. You know what I asked for. What I still want."

He is nice enough this time not to mention that he knows I am tempted.

"You told me you can't take the gift back. Can you take away the curse you added?" If he can remove the caveat, the doubt and refusal to cooperate that now meet my attempts to change fate, I might agree to his terms. It would be worth it to never watch the same disaster twice again. To never have to watch someone get hurt. Mom. Whoever is in the white shirt. And it would be so easy to give in to what he wants. The temptation burns in me.

"No." The single word is a sigh in my ear. Tears push against the inside of my lids. I will see awful things happen forever. I will be forced to watch them play out in reality. Forever.

Apollo's lifts his hand to cup my cheek. I resist the urge to nestle into it like a cat. "But I could add another layer, another modifier, that would make things better."

The fire surges in me, pushes me up onto my toes and into him. My arm slips around his neck. The consequences can't be any worse than what I got for kissing him. Apollo wraps his other arm around me. I feel the same fire burning in him.

I turn my head, bring my lips close to his. Just before I seal my fate, whatever that may be, I stop. Logic barges through the flames. "Wait. What would you do to make things right?" My eyes are now open wide, searching his face for what I desperately want to hear.

Apollo takes in a breath. "I was hoping you wouldn't ask. I'm not sure."

I withdraw my arm, drop back onto my heels and pull away. He has put out the fire.

"I'm sure I can figure something out. I am a god, you know." He gives me a crooked grin. His charm bounces off me like stones.

"I'm not sure you can figure it out. I'm not sure you would even really try." I frown and shake my head. "Why did you give me the gift in the first place? Why did you send the snakes?"

Apollo shrugs. "I get bored. Interacting with mortals gives me something a little unpredictable to deal with. So sometimes I visit them, or send them gifts. Then I get to watch what they do with the gifts."

I am a toy to him. A plaything to manipulate. "But why me?"

"I already told you I didn't really choose you. Your dad did when he pulled your brother free first."

The thought of Nik in my current situation is terrifying. He is too much of a dreamer to deal with the visions, to deal with the gods. I blow out a hard sigh, pushing away the thought. But I still want to know why this man chose my family. "Okay. Why did you send the snakes to us?"

Again, the shrug. "I don't know. I guess because you are twins." He pauses for a moment. "I'm a twin, too, you know."

"I forgot about that." I had forgotten Apollo had a twin sister. But I don't think it matters. His sister has nothing to do with his twisted form of entertainment.

"Wait, do you do this to all twins?" I'm horrified at the thought of how many people Apollo might be toying with. I hope there are others like me. I recognize that I am a mess.

Apollo gives a quick shake of his head. "Just the ones I find intriguing."

"Have you been watching us?"

"Only since I gave you the gift."

"So how did you know you found us intriguing?" This man is more of a mess than I am.

A shrug. That is the answer I get.

"You're Greek?" he adds a tentative question-answer.

"So basically, you pulled our names out of a hat. Or a toga. Or whatever."

Another shrug.

I liked to pretend my visions were a gift that had meaning. I wilt under the knowledge that the gift is random. A god toying with a mortal.

Apollo and I stare at each other across the foot of space holding us apart. The silence is heavy. We are both waiting. I have no idea for what.

Apollo caves first. He stretches out an arm to reach for me. I hold up my hand to stop him. "My answer is still no."

"Oh, that's really too bad." Apollo's arm sinks slowly back to his side. "We would be amazing together." The truth of his words sizzles on my skin. I step back, trying to remove myself from his pull. He stands still, watching me drift away. "I think you'll change your mind, Kassandra. I may, or may not, be willing to help you when you do." With the twist of a threat, Apollo turns and walks toward the edge of the football field. He leaves me alone. Again.

I pack my bow back into my bag and look around the field one last time before I leave. Peter still sits in the bleachers, his eyes on his book. Did he miss the drama that unfolded down here on the field? Could he have overlooked Shannon's injury and the almost-kiss? Or did he break away from the story on the pages to watch the story right in front of him? I want to call to him and ask. I want to know what he knows, what he saw. But I don't call out. I don't want to know he watched me break down, cry in Apollo's arms. I don't want to know I imagined the arms around me, that I sobbed to myself on the field. It is safer not to ask, to pretend he didn't see a thing.

Chapter Eight

Time flies when you're failing to change fate and being proposi-
tioned by a god. That's how the saying goes, right? I glance at
my phone as I pick up my bag to leave the field. 2:30. How did that
happen? I feel like I've only been at practice for ten minutes. More
than an hour and a half have flown out from under me. And I didn't
shoot a single arrow.

On the other hand, no one was shot by one. That is the single bright
spot in today's dismal practice.

I'm not supposed to be at work for another hour, but the thought
of going home makes my stomach turn over. I don't think I can face my
parents. I can't tell them this story. Not yet. The truth would ride over
my face, give away that I am hiding so much more than I am saying.

I head for Spartan Sweets. I can tell Linda the story. Parts of it.
Maybe. Or I can just drown my sorrows and nerves in a sea of warm
sugar.

The store is empty when I enter. The jingle of the bell over the door
is the only sound. "Linda, it's just me!" I call. I don't want Linda to
come running from the back to help a customer who isn't here.

Linda pops her head through the door to the back of the shop
anyway. "You're early! Couldn't wait to get your hands on the wedding
cake, huh?"

I force a flicker of a smile to move across my face. "Something like that. Practice was cut short today." This is the moment where I should say it. Shannon got hurt at practice. Now with Linda in front of me, I can't tell her. Her comfort would crumble me to dust. I don't deserve it. So I hold the words tight, tuck them inside where they aren't real yet.

"I'm glad you're early. The Tuckers want a million fondant roses. I hate making those. Yours always look so much better than mine." She's right, but I don't say it. Hers would be just as good as mine if she would slow down, get lost in the petals instead of driving through to the next thing.

"I'll be there in a minute, Linda. I just want to clean up first." I hold out my hand as if Linda can see the stains of Shannon's blood splashed on my skin. I am a little surprised my hand is clean.

Linda nods and pulls herself back into the prep room.

I let my bag slide from my shoulder and drop to the ground at my feet. It doesn't take the weight of the day with it. I don't know how to do this. How to be around people.

I want Apollo back. He knows. He gets it. I wouldn't have to tell him the story, gloss over my failure, pretend I am not to blame. He understands.

No one else does.

This is my fate. Failure after failure stretches out in front of me. I will have to face them all alone. I can either get used to it or cave and give in to Apollo. Even if I give in though, I still won't be able to prevent what I see from becoming reality.

I pull in a deep breath and move to the bathroom to wash the last two hours away. I splash cold water onto my face, pretending it is the gentle slap of an ocean wave. I pretend it really can take it all away, leave me normal.

I look up to the mirror to check my face. I need to see how much is written there.

I only see myself for a moment. Then I am replaced by a vision of Bridget. I watch a fist fly, crash into her perfect little nose.

I am back in the mirror, the vision gone.

Bridget is going to get punched in the nose. I should be upset at another disaster that I won't be able to prevent. But I can't pretend that a chunk of me won't be thrilled to see her face meet a fist. Bridget has taunted me since kindergarten. It might be nice to see her put in her place, if only for a moment.

I shake that thought away. I am given the visions so that I can change fate. So that I can save lives, and pain. I still believe that, even knowing that Apollo gave me the gift just for fun.

I suppose if given the chance, I will put a barrier between Bridget's nose and the knuckles that hunt them.

But first, I have to make it through this day. No knives for Mom, no arrows for anyone in a white shirt, no fists for Bridget. Am I forgetting anything?

Keeping my secret. Almost forgot that.

I step out of the bathroom with a plan. I will just avoid the topic of practice and Shannon, if possible, deny involvement if I am forced to talk about it.

Lucky for me, Linda has a stream of other topics ready to go. I don't have to do much more than nod or give a token yes of agreement while I spin endless roses for the massive cake Linda is assembling. Five tiers. The bottom tier over three feet across. Linda smooths buttercream, rolls fondant over the tiers, and begins to stack the layers. She doesn't notice I spin roses in silence, not really present in the conversation.

The bell over the front door breaks Linda's stream of chatter. "I'll be right back, Kass. Why don't you take a break? You look beat."

Beaten and broken. That's me.

Linda is through the swinging door before I can answer. The door swings closed, muting the voices on the other side to a faint murmur.

I finish the rose I am working on and stick it into a block of floral foam. The block is covered by a sea of snow-white roses. Over a hundred of them poke out, mounted on thin, tan sticks. They look pure. Clean.

I'm not sure how I made something like that when I am tarnished. I look at my hand again, certain Shannon's blood will be there this time. I have become Lady Macbeth.

I pull a bottle of water out of the fridge. The voices in the front of the store are louder here. They pull me toward the door, but I don't open it.

"Well, I don't know why she wouldn't tell me something so important." Linda's voice is defensive.

"I don't know. But I know it's true." This is a female voice I don't recognize. The tone shifts to something confidential, gossipy. But the volume gets louder. "I saw the ambulance leave the school field myself. The lights were flashing, but the sirens weren't on."

My mouth is stuffed with sandy cotton. They must be talking about Shannon. I pull out my phone, hoping for a message from Shannon. Or coach. Nothing. Is Shannon okay? The ambulance left without sirens. Does that mean Shannon was mostly fine, and they didn't need to be in a big hurry? Does it mean she died? They wouldn't need to hurry then, either. I toss the thought aside. There's just no way that cut would have killed her.

"Did you see Shannon?" Linda asks.

"No. But something happened on that field. The ambulance took Shannon away."

"Have you heard how she's doing? Will she be okay?"

"Rumor is, she cut her arm. Really bad." I hear a sharp inhalation of breath before the next words. "What if they can't fix it? What if they have to amputate? Wouldn't that be a coincidence?" The words are laced with a sick hint of glee. I can imagine the twisted smile on this unknown woman's face.

I cringe. If Shannon loses her arm, it will be my fault. It hasn't occurred to me that the injury could be serious enough to take her arm. I thought she might miss a competition, maybe the rest of the season. Possibly even no more shooting ever. It never crossed my mind that she could lose her arm.

"Well. Hopefully she'll be just fine." Linda's voice is perfectly pleasant on the surface, but I can hear the thread of anger running underneath. "I'm sure Kass knows what happened."

Oh boy. What will I say to Linda? How can I explain why I didn't say anything earlier?

I back away from the door and ponder escaping out the back into the alley. That would only delay the conversation. And add something extra to explain. I stop moving when my back hits the prep counter. The cold steel against my spine gives me strength.

I watch the door swing open. Linda walks through, thankfully alone. Her face is all soft concern. There is no trace of the anger I heard through the door. Apparently, that wasn't for me. "Kass. Honey."

"I'm sorry," I decide a simple apology is my best chance of not spilling the whole truth to Linda. "I just didn't know what to say. I was overwhelmed, I guess."

Linda's eyes shift from me to the field of white roses on the counter next to me. "You came to work, and you made all of those." She shakes her head. "I just blathered on, oblivious." Linda crosses the room and leans her back against the counter next to me. She looks straight ahead, saving me from the weight of her gaze.

I am free to talk. A little. "I saw that her release was loose, and I said something. But I should have pushed harder. I should have reached out and fixed it myself."

"Kass, it's not your fault."

"Maybe." It is my fault. But I can't explain to Linda why the blame belongs only to me. I can't tell her I made a god angry enough to curse me. "I hope she's okay."

"You haven't heard anything?"

"No. All I know is they packed her in an ambulance and took her away." I wipe away the tear that has escaped.

"She'll be all right. Even if she can't shoot her bow for a while. Even if they can't fix her arm. She'll be okay. She'll be alive."

I manage to nod. It's what Linda needs to see. I don't think Shannon would agree with Linda though. Alive is not enough. I wish I could go back in time to one o'clock, to the moment I warned Shannon her strap wasn't right. I want to reach out, cinch the strap tighter with my own hand. Shannon would have been annoyed, upset she had been touched, but her arm would not be ripped open. She would be whole.

Linda turns her head to look at me. "Why don't you take off, hon? You got a lot of the roses made today. We can finish up tomorrow. Or Monday."

I nod again. I have become a mostly mute bobble-head. I let Linda pull me close in a one-armed sideways hug before I grab my bag and escape outside. Alone I can pretend I don't know, I don't see.

Chapter Nine

I am not in a rush to get home. I don't want to tell my parents what happened to Shannon. They will be full of sympathy, full of concern that something like this will happen to me. I am already short one arm, they'll wonder what I will do if I lose the other one. They won't say it out loud, they never do. But the thought will be there, written on their faces. I will be able to read it in their eyes.

I don't have a choice, though. Coach might call and tell them. He might have already. Or they may have heard the gossip at work. It made it to Linda's shop faster than I could have imagined. I can't assume it will avoid Dad's travel agency or the vet's office. If a miracle does occur, and they don't hear about it, they'll notice when Shannon isn't competing at regionals. They'll see her arm wrapped in bandages.

I need a plan. I need Nik. If I tell him before I see our parents, he might be able to help me steer the conversation, make it not be such a big deal. Or he might blow everything way out of proportion and make it worse. Who am I kidding? It really doesn't matter what Nik says about this, it's going to be a big deal for Mom and Dad.

Home, and outside Nik's bedroom, my hand hesitates before knocking. What if Nik freaks out about this? I need him on my side. Just to know he's there, if nothing else. I tap my knuckles against the door, then turn the handle before he has a chance to answer. The door is nearly ripped out of my hand. Joel's face pops into the opening.

"Kass." He nods at me, then wraps me up in a hug and spins me into Nik's room.

I freeze in his arms. This is such a contrast to the rest of my day. I can't process the pure joy radiating out of Joel. "What are you doing?" eventually tumbles from my mouth.

"It's been a good day. I feel like dancing." Joel settles me onto my feet, then pushes his hair back out of his eyes.

"I'm not sure you can call that dancing." I look to Nik for an explanation. Nik stares at his phone, oblivious to the strange behavior of his friend. I turn back to Joel. "Are you staying for dinner?" He would be a perfect distraction.

But he shakes his head. "Nope. I've got a date."

That explains it. The overabundance of energy is Joel excited for a date. No wonder I was confused, I've never seen him like this before. He's never had a date before. That I know of, at least.

"Really?" I ask. "With....."

"Top secret. Can't tell you."

I am drowning in secrets. Mine and everyone else's. Mine win, I can't force myself to focus on anyone else's. "Okaaaay. Have fun?"

Joel nods and waves a hand between Nik and his phone to say goodbye before walking out the door and bouncing down the hall.

I flop onto Nik's bed beside him and wait for him to acknowledge my presence. My hand drifts to a loose curl, weaving it around my fingers like a cat's cradle. I sigh. Loudly. Nik continues to stare at his phone. I free my fingers from my hair and reach out to Nik, work my fingers into the tender space under his ribs.

He tries to slap my hand away without looking away from his phone, but I am persistent. We have played this game before. I always win. Eventually.

I manage to knock the phone from his hand to the floor. I dive for it. Nik is faster. He throws his whole body on top of the phone to keep me away from it. The entire scuffle is silent until it is broken by Nik.

"Ow! Get off me!" he yells when I land on top of him and crush his arms underneath his body.

I slide off onto the floor and sit back on my heels. I have his attention. "What are you looking at on there?"

Nik remains sprawled on the floor, his phone underneath his chest, his head turned to the side to see me. "I was watching a symphony performance."

"With no sound? What's the point of that?"

Nik shifts to sit cross-legged on the floor. "If the musicians are really into a piece, you can almost hear the music just watching them. It plays on their faces, in their bodies. It's pretty amazing."

Nik is the same way when he plays. Even when I can hear the music coming from his cello, I can see it in him, too.

"So why hide it from me?"

"It's kind of weird." He gives me a half smile, then looks down at the phone again. "And I wanted to finish watching."

"I think Joel is starting to infect you with odd. Hey!" I put my hand over his phone, blocking his view of the screen. "Can I talk to you for a minute? With you looking at me and at least pretending to pay attention?"

Nik looks up as if he can see the sky through the ceiling of his room, then back down at his phone. He touches the screen, then tucks it under his right thigh. "You have my complete and undivided attention, oh, great Kassandra."

I ignore his sarcasm. "Something happened today. I need to tell Mom and Dad before they hear it from someone else, but I'm worried they'll freak out on me. Or just freak out on the inside and hide it from me."

"I have no idea what you just said. How about you just tell me what happened?" Nik's face is pained. It is clearly taking everything he has to continue listening to me instead of returning to the video.

"At practice today. Shannon got hurt."

"Wait," Nik really looks at me. His eyes meet mine and everything. "What happened? Did you shoot her?"

A flicker of a golden arrow brushes across my mind. I wave it away.

"No!" I smack his shoulder. "I wouldn't do that. I don't think she'd shoot me, either."

Nik raises an eyebrow.

"Maybe." I'm no more sure than he is. "Anyway. Her release strap was loose. Which changed the angle or alignment of her bow or something. When she released the arrow, the string and nocking point hit her arm and cut her open."

"Holy shit! Why didn't I go to your practice today?"

"Because you never do. It was crazy. Coach took her off in an ambulance."

"Was there blood everywhere?"

I frown at his uber-boyness. "Yeah. She was bleeding. But you're missing the point."

Nik shakes his head, his eyes wide. To him blood is the point.

"Mom and Dad are going to be worried all over again about me doing this. Shannon has both of her arms, she's been shooting longer than me, and she still got hurt. I doubt she'll be able to compete in two weeks. Maybe not for the rest of the season. She could have permanent nerve damage or something."

"Wait. You think they're going to tell you you can't shoot anymore?" Somehow, I have left Nik behind.

"I doubt they'll say that, but I guess it's an option." I look down at my hand where it sits safely in my lap. "I'm more worried they'll just think I shouldn't be doing it anymore. That they'll doubt me but not tell me. I think they'll pretend to be cautiously supportive on the outside, when they really want me to quit. When really they think I can't do it."

"Why would they think you can't do it?" Nik looks genuinely perplexed, like my words are strung together in an order that makes no sense. "You've been doing this for five years, Kass. We all know you can do it."

I want to believe him. "Sometimes when Mom and Dad look at me, even when you look at me, I see doubt in your eyes."

"You gotta stop it, Kass. We don't doubt you, not even a little. You've shown us time after time there isn't anything that can stop you. Nothing you can't do. You're like Super Woman." Nik pulls himself from the floor to his feet and tucks his phone into his back pocket. He holds out a hand to me. "Let's go see if dinner is ready. I'm starving."

I grab his hand and pull myself up. I give Nik a speedy hug and a smacking kiss on the cheek, then run out the door before he can inflict revenge.

Halfway down the stairs, I slow. I can hear Mom and Dad in the kitchen. They are little more than a murmur, but they sound happy. I don't want to barge in with news that will turn their happiness to worry.

"It'll be fine, Kass," Nik says behind me. "They'll be concerned because someone got hurt, and they don't want you to get hurt. But they're not going to tell you to stop. They won't wish you would decide to stop on your own."

I wish that was the only thing weighing on me. I wish I didn't have to keep the visions secret from my parents, from Nik. I don't like lying to them. It's just a lie of omission. But this lie of omission is huge.

Nik nudges me to the side and darts down the steps ahead of me. I trail in his wake. I stop near the kitchen and pick up Luna. The instant purring is almost as good at soothing my nerves as the sound of the ocean. I take a deep breath, set down the cat, and face my family.

The instant I cross the threshold, my phone buzzes in my pocket. I pull the phone free. A text from Coach.

Shannon is on her way home. She's okay, I guess. Her arm will heal eventually. No competition for her anytime soon. YOU have practice next Saturday. Get some extra time in on your own this week, as well.

I push out a wave of stale, stressed air, then text back. *Glad she's okay. See you next week.*

"What was the big sigh?" Mom asks. I hadn't realized my exhalation was that extreme. But Nik, Mom, and Dad are all staring at me.

My eyes dart to Nik. He gives a tiny nod. He thinks I should just spill it. So I do. "That was Coach. Something happened at practice today, but things will be okay in the end. I think."

"What happened?" Mom drops the hot pad and pizza cutter next to the pizza and moves around the island to stand in front of me. Her fingers remain safe today. My vision was clearly a knife, not a pizza cutter.

"Shannon hurt her arm. Her release was a little loose, and it made the string hit her arm when she fired." And it's my fault. I manage to keep the last bit in my head.

"That doesn't sound like a big deal," Dad says.

"The nock, Dad." Blank stare. "It's the hard plastic part the arrow sits in. It hit her hard enough that it cut her arm."

Mom's hand flies to her mouth. I bite my lip. This was what I didn't want. Mom's concern, her mom-vision playing all the horrible things that could happen to me. As if I haven't already survived one of the most horrible things that could happen to a person.

I watch Mom fight the urge to wrap me up in her arms. The urge to tuck me away somewhere where bad things can't get to me. If she decides to do it, I'll probably let her. But she fights her way through it and slowly lowers her hand. "Will she be okay?" Mom's voice is surprisingly even.

"Yeah. It will heal, Coach said. But she can't compete in regionals."

"When is that again?" Dad asks.

I was right. It's been one day, and he has forgotten already. "Two weeks from today, Dad."

"No pressure on you, huh?" Dad slides the pizza cutter through the pizza in front of him on the island. "Now that you're the only one from Delphi Springs competing, Coach is going to expect you to win."

"George, hush," Mom says. "I'm sure Coach won't expect you to win just because Shannon can't compete." She sends a wave of support to me with a smile. "As always, just do your best." She really is taking this far better than I had hoped. I don't see a hint of stop shooting anywhere on her face.

"You should take advantage of Shannon not being there. This might be your only chance to take first," Nik says.

I grab the hot pad and throw it at Nik's head. "Thanks for the support, jerk."

"Oh, Kass," Mom turns the conversation before things get too far. "I almost forgot. I got a call today about the Greek goddess competition. The photo shoot is next Saturday at four. You're supposed to meet outside of Sponge Brothers."

I groan. "Do I have to?"

"It's an honor to be nominated, Kass. Enjoy it." Mom rubs a hand up and down my arm, then turns to the pizza. She won't have to deal with the stares.

"Toga. Toga." Nik begins a slow chant.

"And you doubt I'm the older twin?" I ask him.

Chapter Ten

I miss the thing I am now afraid of. I haven't had a vision since I saw Bridget punched in the face. That was a week ago. I already have three dangling visions, three futures waiting for me to change them. And yet I am worried about this week of no visions.

Does my lack of visions mean everyone else I can touch is safe? Or does it mean I am just being denied the chance to help them? At least if I were having visions, I would know what was happening. And how much of it is my fault.

Today I am faced with the thing I know for certain is my fault.

Shannon is at practice. She sits on a bench on the side of the field, watching every move I make. She doesn't say a word. Just sits. Stares. Judges.

I avoid eye contact.

Coach is extra harsh today. He doesn't need to divide his criticism between two archers, so he piles it all on me. The weight of his expectations rests on my shoulders from the moment I pick up my bow.

"Arms up, Pitera! What's with the spaghetti arms?"

"Line it up! Hips! Shoulders!"

"Up! Shit. I'm tired of repeating myself!"

I am crushed under the two-hour onslaught of critical exclamations. My eyes are exhausted from watching for the appearance of a golden arrow.

It finally comes to an end. I have made it through Coach's battering, now it is time to face Shannon's.

"You better win next week." Her voice is level but loaded. "You don't have to worry about me, so there's no excuse not to."

Oh, good. No pressure. "I'm so sorry you can't compete, Shannon. Really. I wish you could."

Shannon gives one single nod. I can't tell if it is an acceptance of my apology or an acknowledgment that the blame for her injury belongs to me. "See you Saturday," is all she says. It does not clear up my uncertainty.

"Hey, Kassandra." Coach heads toward me. His eyes don't meet mine. He looks instead at my shoes, my bow propped against my bag. This is what always happens when the bow isn't in my hand. He loses all his coach-ness. It is like he sees me as two different people. When I hold my bow, he sees a strong, capable archer. Without my bow, he sees a broken, disabled waif.

Without my bow, his eyes drift from my stump to my hand, never to my face. His words soften; his criticism laced with apology. "You should maybe try to put in some extra hours this week. You're dropping your bow with every release. If you wanna hit the bull, you need to keep it up." This from the man who just spent two hours yelling curses at me.

Coach starts to walk away, then turns on his heel. This time he looks at my right hand. Still not my face. "Forgot to tell you. I took on another student. A transfer from out of state. He'll be competing on Saturday, so you can meet him then. If he's not in your classes." Coach chuckles. "His name's Apollo, if you can believe that!" He turns away again. "See you Saturday, kid."

I am left standing on the field. Alone again. Stunned again. It can't be him. The Apollo I know isn't a teenager, a student. He doesn't look like he could pass for one, really. His eyes are too wise. His face and body too perfect. He would draw too much attention to pass the scrutiny. Coach's new student probably has parents who are obsessed with mythology. Or maybe speed skating.

I haven't seen my Apollo since last week when I stood here sobbing in his arms. Why am I thinking of him as "mine?" I want to hope he will stay away, leave me alone forever. But I can't deny there is a part of me that wishes he will reappear, offer something to fix everything he has broken.

My phone chimes from my bag. I pick it up. A schedule reminder. The photo-shoot.

Crap.

I send Julie a text. *Are you ready?*

Julie's reply is almost instantaneous. YES!! I'M HERE ALREADY. WHERE ARE YOU?

Just leaving practice. There in 5.

I drop my phone back into my bag, tuck my arrows into the quiver and nestle my bow in my bag. I wish I had a little bit of Julie's excitement for this.

I am one of six girls nominated for Greek goddess. It is supposed to be an honor. It is supposed to make me feel special. It just makes me feel stared at. The only good news is this is the last time I can be nominated. The goddess has to be a junior or senior. I will graduate in May and be free from this particular version of torture.

I join Julie and the other four nominees in front of Sponge Brothers. I look at the group. This is sad. I am probably going to win the crown again this year, even though I would rather any of these girls take it instead. Our group is varied, but the voting will go like it always goes. People will vote for the girl who is the best match to their mental image of a classical Greek goddess.

I look Greek. Dark curly hair, large brown eyes, a hint of olive in my skin. Julie is Puerto Rican, too tan and curvy. Mirabelle has gorgeous ebony skin framed by clipped dark hair. Kendra looks like a tiny blond pixie. Janie has dark curly hair like mine, but it frames creamy, pale skin dotted with freckles and bright green eyes. Leilah is another blond, but unlike Kendra, she is super tall and muscular. In my opinion, she looks the most like a goddess, but she looks like a California goddess, not the Greek goddess Delphi Springs thinks they need.

Take me out of this, and you would see next spring's prom court. They are all beautiful. They are all popular. They all deserve the title of goddess.

I am inadequate. I will win anyway. It burns in my throat like a bitter pill stuck after swallowing.

I am tempted to drop out, refuse to have my picture taken today. Dad would be crushed. He loves Delphi Fest. He loves everything about our family's Greek heritage. I will suffer through this and try to let myself be the queen he sees in me.

***

I saw this coming.

It is god-awful early o'clock on Monday morning. I am in anatomy and physiology, my first class of the day on blue days.

Apollo just walked through the door and sat at the table behind me.

I think at first maybe he got a haircut or just lost some of his tan. I can't quite figure out what is different. He looks a little younger, really my age now. He looks dimmer. As if he took the god in him and dialed it down. He is still ridiculously attractive, but slightly shorter, slightly less muscular, slightly less astounding. This Apollo can pass for a high school student. He still draws stares. He is still too gorgeous. But the stares are not laced with disbelief.

Every female eye in the room is fixed on his face. Most of the male eyes, too. He does not wilt under the attention, like I would. It feeds him. I am turned sideways in my seat so I can watch him soak it up. And so I can keep an eye on him. All my visions end in disaster. This will be no different. But this one is going to hurt. Unless I can wiggle my way out of it.

Stopping this vision might be a two-fer. I'm pretty sure today is why Bridget gets a fist to her perfect face.

I pivot back to face the front of the room, my eyes fixed firmly on my open notebook. I can hear snippets of whispers around me. "Hot." "Eyes." "Curls." "Ass." That last one makes me look up. Bridget is turned fully around in her seat at the table next to mine. She isn't even pretending not to stare. If there weren't an audience, I'm pretty sure she would literally jump on him. I'm not sure the audience will be enough to hold her back for long.

My chair scootches forward. I turn my head, casting my sight back over my shoulder. I can barely see Apollo out of the corner of my eye. I refuse to give him my attention when he has so much else to choose from.

"Kass." I see his mouth open to say more. I am saved by the bell. Well, the arrival of Ms. Rosnick. She floats in, her skirt a swirl of fluttering layers around her.

"Good morning, class. I hope you all had a marvelous weekend."

She is greeted by a mixture of grunts, groans, and murmurs. Without looking behind me, I can tell the true focus of the class is still on the man behind me. Ms. Rosnick is going to have a hard time teaching this group anything today.

"I need a volunteer."

This might be the only thing she could say that could compete with Apollo's presence. Along with everyone else in the room, all my attention is now on Ms. Rosnick, though I do not look directly at her. I do not want to be chosen. Especially today. In front of him.

"Kassandra?" Ms. Rosnick is now beside my table, looking down at me. "Can I have your assistance, please?"

I look up at her and slap a smile on my face. "I think we have a new student today. Maybe he should help? So everyone can get a chance to get to know him?" They're all staring at him, anyway, I want to add. Might as well have them stare at the front of the room.

I can see her consider this for a moment. And then she shakes her head. There goes my only shot of preventing what comes next. Sorry Bridget. Sorry future Me.

"I wouldn't want to do that to someone on their first day. Let's give him a chance to settle in a bit before I make him be my guinea pig."

Ms. Rosnick turns and drifts to the front of the room. This is my cue to stand and follow her. I am very careful not to look at Apollo when I do. I can't watch him watch me fail. This time I won't be able to cry in his arms afterward, either. There will be too many eyes.

The front of the room is a terrifying place. I am looking out at a sea of intense scrutiny mixed with complete disregard. For now. Soon it will shift to full scrutiny.

"All right everyone. Today we are looking at anatomical terms of movement. Kassandra, can you raise your arms to the sides, please."

I lift my arms, forming a lopsided T with my body.

"This is abduction. Abduction moves a limb away from the midline of the body. Kassandra, arms down."

I drop my arms.

"This is adduction. Adduction moves a limb toward the midline."

Bridget raises her hand. Here it comes. I feel the muscles in my neck and shoulders tighten in a move of unintentional elevation.

"Bridget?"

I cannot look at Bridget. I will not look at Apollo. The only safe place for my eyes is the floor. Maybe if no one can see my eyes, no one will know when Bridget's words cut me, make me bleed.

"So, if a limb is mutated and smaller than it should be, doesn't the word get shortened? Like abdie and addie maybe?"

There is total silence for two seconds. Two seconds of forever. Then a titter. A giggle. An outbreak of chatter.

I don't let myself flinch. I am a statue, carved to look only at the floor at my feet. I can feel the chaos unspooling around me. At its center, I feel the calm core that is Apollo. Without looking, I can tell he is still in his seat, his eyes watching me watch the floor. More entertainment for him, I guess.

"Bridget. Office. Now." If I am a statue of stone, Ms. Rosnick's voice is cold steel. She is pissed.

So am I. Oddly I have no desire to punch Bridget, though. Whose fist is fated for her?

I feel a gentle hand on my arm. I pry my eyes from the floor to look at the hand, then trail up the arm to the face it belongs to. Ms. Rosnick's face is the wreckage left behind by a tornado. She didn't see this coming like I did. "Have a seat, Kass." Her voice drops to a whisper. "I'm sorry."

I shake my head once and move quickly to my chair. The only face I let myself glance at is Apollo's. I was right. He is focused very intently on me. He's not even watching the scene around us. I don't think he hears the laughter and jokes that swirl through the air. I am entertaining enough.

I wish he had given me the gift of a deadly glare instead of visions. He would be dust.

I sink into my seat and look straight ahead. Even though I knew this was going to happen, it still hurts. No amount of preparation would have made this okay. The only bright light is that I know someone has my back. Fate will pay Bridget a visit.

"Okay everyone. Settle down please." Ms. Rosnick gradually pulls the class back to her. "I expect better of all of you. You are not children. Please do not act like it in my room."

She picks up a stack of manila envelopes from her desk and glides around the room, dropping them onto the tables. "Partners, please."

There is an immediate scuffle and sliding of chairs. The room shifts around me as everyone tries to get the partner they want. I am still.

Ms. Rosnick turns at the front of the room to check on the partnering. "Kass, could you work with Apollo, please?"

Shit. I had hoped he would be snatched up by one of the greedy-eyed monsters. Instead, we are the only two singles left in the room. I give a nod. It can't really get any worse, can it?

When I turn around, Apollo has already spilled the contents of the envelope onto his table. A handful of notecards, each with a single word. A sheet of instructions.

"So," he says.

"So."

"That was harsh."

"Yep. It was also your fault."

His eyes narrow. "My fault?"

I glance around. Everyone is focused on their cards, trying to figure out what Ms. Rosnick wants us to do. I drop my voice to a whisper anyway. "I had a vision this morning. I knew what Bridget was going to say. But your curse kept me from avoiding it."

"Oh."

His eyes drift away from me. He looks upset. Maybe he's finally starting to realize what he has done.

"I'm sorry."

"Whatever." His apologies do nothing. It changes nothing.

"I also had a vision of her getting punched in the face. So, there's that."

Apollo's eyes crash back to mine.

"Are you going to be the one who punches her?" I ask.

His eyes widen, then narrow again as if he is considering it.

"I don't think so. That's a little too hands-on for me."

I start to laugh but cut myself off. His face is all business. He is not joking.

"Do you want to go first?"

"What?"

Apollo is looking at the instruction sheet. "We're supposed to draw a card and then act out the word."

"I've had enough acting today, thanks."

Apollo stands up beside the table. Most of the class is now out of their seats, pronating, depressing, and supinating around me. He lifts one foot off the ground and points his toe to the ground.

"Plantarflexion," I say.

He lifts his toes to the ceiling.

"Dorsiflexion."

Apollo drops back into his seat and pushes the cards aside. "You don't need the practice. You know this stuff."

"I did my homework."

"Hm." Apollo leans back in his chair, tipping it onto the back two legs. I can almost imagine he is just the new guy in class. He is doing a great impression of one. I want to pretend he is just a guy, not a god I have kissed and cried on. Not a man who has gifted me, then cursed me.

"Let's talk about something else then. Today's events."

"What do you mean?" I'm not sure what he wants me to say. He saw the whole thing. I would love to pretend it didn't happen.

"You say it's my fault. But you deserved the curse."

"Excuse me?"

"You didn't give me what I want." Now he looks more like a little boy denied access to the cookie jar than a high school guy or a god.

I lean close so I can give my words very little air. "You wanted me to have sex with you. I said no."

Apollo drops his chair back on all fours to complement my body language. We are both leaning over the table, our heads mere inches apart. "I asked for compensation for my gift."

"A gift you gave me when I was a baby. A gift I didn't ask for, didn't want."

"Doesn't matter. A gift is a gift. A gift from a god is an extraordinary gift."

"In your opinion."

"It let you change fate. It lets you save lives."

"And you took it away. That was your choice."

"I offered to try to fix it. You said no to that too."

"Because you didn't have a plan. You weren't really sure you could fix anything."

"Yeeessss..."

"Has that changed?"

"No."

Silent staring ensues. He breaks eye contact first. I feel his eyes trail over my face, over the rest of me. I practice statue mode again. I watch his face. He softens. I want to reach out and brush my fingers over his skin. I want to feel his warmth. I want to let him care.

He knows there is a battle in me. The parts that want to give him what he wants just to share it with him war with the parts that know things will only get worse if I do.

"You're going to cave, Kassandra. Someday. You will realize you can't save everyone. You can't even save yourself. You will want my help. You will need me."

His words are a punch to my stomach. This I did not see coming. My vision left out the best worst part. I am pushed back in my chair, out of his space and into myself. He is wrong. I can save myself, not that I need saving. I can save everyone else, too. I just have to find a way around the curse. I don't need him. I won't.

***

I don't want to save Bridget.

I don't want to punch her myself, either.

The truth is, I would love to sit on the brick benches that surround the statue of Zeus out front and watch her get pummeled. All the joy of her getting a little pay-back for the hell she dishes out with none of the blood or bruises on my hands.

This is my plan when the final bell rings. I head for the front doors, my skin hungry for sunshine, my heart hungry for vengeance.

I'm not sure if Bridget will get her punch today, but I plan to have a ring-side seat just in case.

I am only two steps out the door when a hand grabs my arm and pulls me behind a pillar.

"Kass. Why didn't you tell me what happened?"

My best friend's face is curled into frustrated anger. I'm not sure if she's mad at me or at Bridget. Or something else entirely.

"It wasn't worth my time. It was just Bridget being Bridget." I don't bother to tell Julie that I already knew there would be a penalty other than the principal's office for Bridget.

"I'm sick of her shit. I'm sick of everyone excusing her. As if the fact that she's a bitch makes her daily attacks okay. We should just take it and bow down to Queen Bridget. Fuck that." Julie is so worked up that her words tumble over each other, fighting to get out of her mouth first.

I start to say something, then stop. I'm not sure what the words were. Calm down? It's not a big deal? Julie's right. We let her get away with it. This is when I realize whose fist was in my vision. I should have known.

Julie takes my silence as consent. Or support. I'm not quite willing to admit that's what it is. Julie turns her back to me and scans the student bodies spread around Zeus. Without seeing Julie's face, I know when she finds Bridget. Julie sinks back onto her heels for a minute. A huge intake of air stiffens her spine and sets her head.

She is off before I can even consider stopping her. All thoughts of a ring-side seat are gone. I step into the ring a moment behind Julie, follow her into the heart of what I know is going to be a fight.

Julie stops less than a foot from Bridget, all her weight shifted forward onto her toes. If it weren't for the anger streaming off her, it might look like Julie was leaning in for a kiss.

Bridget turns a saccharine sweet smile to Julie. "Hi, Julie. How are you?"

Julie drops back onto her heels. The sweetness has knocked her anger off kilter, squelched it under a blanket of confusion.

Bridget's eyes drift past Julie's shoulder. One carefully sculpted brow perks when Bridget's eyes find their target. Me.

"I see you brought your pet with you today."

Bridget is very good at causing the calm before the storm. I think that's her favorite part. The moment when everyone around her takes a pause to appreciate what she has just done. The moment before everything explodes.

"She's not my pet. She's my best friend. You need to find someone else to pick on."

Julie has fallen victim to Bridget's shift. I'm not sure if Julie is even aware of the shift, or if Bridget knew she was causing a shift. But with that one sentence, she pushed Julie's focused anger off the big picture. She pushed all of Julie's focus onto me.

"I don't need you to fight my battles for me, Julie." My words are soft, meant only for Julie. I want her to turn to me for a moment. I want a chance to remind her of the bigger issue. Bridget is a bitch. That's the real issue.

Julie is not the only person to hear my words.

"Yeah," Bridget says. "She might need you to cut her steak, but she could just shoot me with her bow if she wanted."

Julie's fist flies.

This time Bridget is in the center of the storm she has created. Judging by the shriek and look on her face, I don't think she enjoys it much.

Welcome to our world, Bridget.

Chapter Eleven

I spend the rest of the week pretending Apollo does not sit behind me in anatomy. Apollo spends the rest of the week avoiding
Bridget. Bridget spends the rest of the week in detention; a bandage
splashed across her face. Julie also spends the week in detention, but
her face is splashed with a smile. It is a long four days of pretending
not to feel Apollo's eyes on me, pretending I have everything under
control.

Saturday morning is bright and clear. I am not. I stand on our back
porch, letting the sun soak into my skin. I listen to the faint sound of
the ocean washing over me with the breeze. The early morning air has a
bit of a bite. I walk back inside and let my eyes roll. Nik is still upstairs.

"Nik!" I yell from the bottom of the stairs. "You're going to make
me late!"

"Kass. Calm down." Mom is in the living room. She is curled up
on the couch with a cup of coffee. Why isn't she ready to go, either?
"We've got an hour or so before we need to leave."

"I want to be there early, Mom. I need to be sure I'm warm and
ready to go." I am nervous. I am antsy. I want it to be done.

"If we leave in hour, you'll have plenty of time. The competition
doesn't start until eleven, hon."

I pace between the stairs and the coach. Luna meows at me from her perch on the stair railing.

"Kass." Mom's tone is sharp. "Go take a walk. Please."

That is a good idea. I can go get rid of some of this electric energy charging through me. "Thirty minutes," I say. "Can you please get Nik moving?"

"We'll be ready. Stop worrying." Mom smiles, then turns her eyes back to the book stretched across her lap.

I resist the urge to snap the book shut, run up the stairs and drag Nik down. I leave the house instead.

The instant I am outside, I hear the rolling waves. Their song travels the two blocks that separate our house from the beach. They call to me. I answer, moving directly toward them. I stop at the boundary between sidewalk and sand. I toe off my shoes and leave my socks dangling out of them.

I pause at the border between wet and dry. Air holes pop to the surface of the saturated sand, revealing the presence of crabs and other critters. I won't dig them up today. Today I just want to share the sand with them. I burrow down with my toes. The soppy, scratchy sand squelches up between them. I breathe out, blow the tension away.

This works every time. Every time I am wound too tight the beach undoes me. I root myself in the sand, feel the water wash up onto my legs. Salt sprays up from the ocean and floats in the breeze that brushes across me like a caress. I close my eyes, let the briny air filter in and cleanse me from the inside out.

The muscles in my back and shoulders finally unkink. I haven't realized how much I have been carrying there for the last week.

I open my eyes and look out at the wind-tossed sea. Let it be all chaos. I am calm.

Centered again, I turn, retrieve my socks and shoes, and walk home.

Nik is downstairs eating a bowl of cereal when I enter the house. His earbuds are plugged into his ears as usual. Mom is packing a bag of snacks and drinks. Dad is on the living room floor, doing his version of sit-ups. I smile. Everything is exactly as it should be.

I hold onto my peace through the drive to Sarasota. I hold onto it through the hugs from my family, their ascent into the stands surrounding the huge field. I hold onto it through my warm-up. I hold onto it through a scan of the competitors for white shirts and golden arrows. I hold onto it through Shannon's arrival.

I lose it when Coach Hamilton arrives.

He has his new student with him. The one I convinced myself was not who I knew he was. He looks different somehow, but there is no doubt in my mind. My Apollo. The man I kissed. The man who cursed me. The man who now sits behind me in anatomy.

"Kass, this is Apollo. Apollo, Kass." Coach rushes through the introduction, eager to get Apollo shooting. I don't have time to collect myself and stutter a hello before Coach drags Apollo past me to join the other male competitors.

Apollo turns slightly as he walks past and locks eyes with me. He winks, then turns back to walk beside Coach, chats with him about glow-in-the-dark nocks.

I am frozen again. All the tension I washed away at the beach crashes back into me, a tsunami of frustrated fear. Why is he here? Why is he everywhere? What does he want from me? I don't know what he's up to, what he hopes to gain by masquerading as a high school student and competing in an archery competition.

Shannon saves me. "Kass! Hello?" The hand of her uninjured arm snakes out to pinch my bicep. "Get your shit together, girl. You don't have time to be all spacey right now. Yeah, he's hot as hell. Don't let that beat you."

Once I manage to focus on her, Shannon keeps talking. "Close your eyes and listen." I do as she says, unable to act on my own. "Whatever it is that's running around in your head right now, I want you to visualize it standing in front of you. See yourself reach out, crush it, squash it down until it fits into a tiny little box. I want you to lock that tiny little box. Put that box in your bag and save it for later. You can deal with whatever is inside when this meet is over. Got it?"

I pull in a deep breath and let it drift away. I open my eyes and nod. I can do this. Ignore Apollo today. Deal with all the rest later. "Thanks, Shannon. I'm ready." All I have to do is stay away from Apollo, avoid looking at him. Avoid being close enough to touch or smell him. The field is set up for males and females to compete separately. This should be easy.

Shannon moves away and settles on the sidelines to watch the action. I check my bow one more time and cinch my release strap tightly onto my stump. I check the fit three times. I can't help but imagine the nock slicing into my flesh like it did Shannon. I keep all my attention directed within. I don't watch the other competitors. I don't make eye contact with anyone. I wait, listen only to the names that are called, until I hear my own.

I step up to the mark and look down the length of the field to the target. Red and white stripes ring a yellow dot. I look down briefly to connect the release and arrow to my bow string. My right hand holds the grip and raises the bow as my stump pulls up and back. I use the release to draw the bow string back until it locks.

I stand. My attention narrowed to the yellow dot fifty feet away. Now I am a modern-day statue of Artemis. I know there must be hundreds of eyes on me right now, but I block them all.

I take in a deep breath, then release it. I press my jaw against the release trigger and send the arrow flying. I hear Coach's voice from the sidelines. A single "Yes!" confirms my shot is good. I watch the arrow sail straight and true, until it comes to a halt in the center of the yellow dot.

I draw again. The next arrow lands in the white circle just outside the yellow. The third is again in the yellow.

I lower my arm and turn. I finally let myself see the huge field around me. It is split in two. Each side has two straight rows of targets at the far end. Each side is lined with a thick band of competitors and coaches. The stands are nowhere near full, but still hold at least a thousand people.

I forget to avoid the other side of the field. My eyes travel there, find Apollo, meet his gaze. We stare at each other, oblivious to the bodies around us, moving between us. He looks away first. It feels like a victory. He bends to grab his bow and moves to his mark.

My eyes follow him, then my body. I nod to people who offer congratulations as I move to rest my bow on the rack. My eyes keep tabs on Apollo as I join the crowd on the men's half of the field.

Apollo lifts his bow in his left hand. His right hand draws back the string. His bow is stunning. Confusing. It is different than any I have seen before in competition. Or anywhere else. I am surprised he is allowed to use it here, impressed it passed inspection. It has cams, like all the compound bows around me, but the string runs straight from cam to cam, without crossing over. It looks like a mix between a compound bow and a recurve bow. Most of the bows here are black, white, or camo. Apollo's is bright gold. I squint my eyes. I swear I catch the glint of sunlight reflecting off the bow, as if it is made of pure gold.

The arrow braced to fire is the golden arrow from my vision. The shaft shines in the sun. Only the fletching is a different color. They are white, pure, like the feathers of a dove. This beautiful thing is destined to pierce someone's flesh. Apollo will shoot someone.

As Apollo draws, he glances at the target for a split second, then turns his head to the crowd. His eyes find me. Without blinking or looking away, he completes his draw, then releases the arrow. I can't pull my eyes from his, can't watch the arrow find flesh. There is a gasp from the crowd. A wave of applause and cheers follow. The arrow found the target. This time.

Apollo smiles for me, and winks again. The connection between us is broken when Coach Hamilton attacks Apollo, wrapping his arms around my god.

I turn away. What was that? Nobody pulls trick shots in competition. It is too risky. You could be way off and hurt someone. Which is what my vision told me would happen. You could be just a little off and lose the competition. Was that shot for me? To show me what he is capable of? To prove he is still a god despite his dimmed appearance? Was it a threat? A promise of what is to come? I don't know what it was. But I know I don't like it.

I move back to the women's side of the competition field and take a few minutes to recover my focus. There are still several rounds of shooting to go. And the bar has just been raised.

***

I keep my back to the men's side for the remainder of the competition. I have to force myself to keep my focus on my bow, my hand, my release.

I can't watch Apollo shoot someone here.

I can't do anything to stop it, either.

I push the fragments of vision that pop to the surface of my mind back in Shannon's little box. Over and over.

I manage to avoid seeing Apollo again until the awards ceremony at the end of the day. Maybe only because he lets me avoid him. He wants me to stew over what he is, what he can do.

I win the women's division, but barely. My score is 273 to the second-place score of 271. If Shannon had been able to compete, there's no way I would have won.

Apollo would have won the men's division no matter who else was here. His score was a perfect 300. I've never seen that in competition. It just doesn't happen. Everyone fumbles. The breeze picks up. Dogs bark. Everyone misses the mark, at least once.

Coach Hamilton is bouncing like a little boy. He pulls Apollo and me to his sides and demands photos be taken. I try to look happy. I just won. But Apollo's presence just a foot away, separated from me only by Coach's body, weighs on me. It tarnishes my win. I manage to free myself from Coach and catch the eye of Nik in the crowd. I need to get out of here, scoot away before I am forced to interact with Apollo again.

I grab my bag and begin threading my way through the crowd. I am so close to escaping when I feel a hand grasp my arm and pull me around. Apollo looks down at me, a wide smile on his face. "Congratulations, Kassandra."

"Thanks. You, too," I say to my shoes. I have spent more time looking at the ground and my feet since I met this man.

He lifts my chin and forces me to meet his gaze. "Meet me at The Springs tonight. Eight o'clock. I need to talk to you."

"What if I say no?" Meetings with Apollo do not end well for me. I don't want to risk another addition to my punishment if I continue to refuse to give him what he wants. I don't want to risk caving and giving him what he wants. But he is here, masquerading as a student and I don't know why.

He tips his head to the side and lets a small smile play across his lips. "You'll be there. You're curious. I can see it in your eyes." This is why I stare at the floor so much. He sees me too well.

His hand is still wrapped around my arm. He releases me and lets his fingers trail down my arm and twine briefly with my fingers before drifting away. I feel the brief contact in every cell of my body, a wave crashing through me.

"I'll see you at eight," he says as he walks away.

We both know he is right.

Chapter Twelve

M y parents insist on a celebration dinner. Without asking where I want to go, Dad steers the car to my favorite restaurant in Delphi Springs. Sponge Brothers Sea Shack is right by the docks. They specialize in seafood pulled out of the ocean that morning. Everything here is amazing.

The entire restaurant smells like the docks. Mostly because one entire wall of the restaurant is made of folding window panels that are open as long as the weather is close to decent. I've never seen them closed. Eating in the restaurant feels like you are eating right on the dock. The briny, fishy aroma washes in with each wave that crashes on the piers outside.

I try to work up some enthusiasm for my win. It really is a big deal. The win at regionals means I am headed to state competition in February. This is the first year I have qualified. Usually, it is Shannon who goes.

The trouble is Apollo. As always. My "date" with him later lurks, hovers over me, pops up every time I manage to tuck it away. His golden arrow glides in front of me every time I blink. I keep my eyes open wide, looking for a white T shirt.

Nik elbows me as we slide into the booth across from our parents. "What is wrong with you?"

I just shake my head and force a smile. I can't even begin to explain.

A waiter walks up to our table; a basket of garlic bread and four waters balanced on his tray. His shirt is white but has a line of buttons up the front. He is safe.

I pull in the aroma of the bread. Way too much garlic for some, but it smells like heaven to me. Maybe the garlic breath will help keep Apollo at a distance later. I tuck him away yet again, shove him down with a piece of bread.

"What are you having, woman of the hour?" Dad asks as he pushes a menu over to me.

I don't even open it.

"Crab legs."

Mom smiles. I watch the worry that has been etched on her face this afternoon slide away.

I never order crab legs. Crab legs are a lot of work. You need a fair amount of strength to crack the shells. Then you have to dig out the tender bits of flesh from the slender, spindly legs. I hate eating them in public. I feel like I'm on display when I do. People stop to watch, curious how the one-handed girl is going to manage to get into them. Like they want to see me fail. Want me to ask my parents to do it for me, like I am a baby.

"That's my girl!" Dad leans across the table and reaches to ruffle my hair. I dodge.

"And I need key lime pie." Just saying the words makes saliva flood into my mouth.

"The champion gets what she wants," Dad says.

"Dad. Enough, please."

"Kass," Mom says. "You should be celebrating your big win."

"I guess it just doesn't feel like a win."

"Why?"

I want to tell them about Apollo, the weight of his presence hanging over me. Not possible. So, I give them a partial truth, the smaller thing that taints the day. "Shannon should have won. She would have won if she had competed today."

"You don't know that."

"I do, Mom. She's better than I am. That's just reality."

Silence falls on the table; a heavy shroud muffles us all. It is briefly broken by our waiter dropping off our drinks and taking our dinner orders.

I feel tears prick at the back of my eyes. I wish I could rewind time, go back to my birthday, back when everything had been my version of normal. Before Apollo arrived and altered my world. "Sorry," I mutter after the waiter leaves us stewing in silence again. "I guess it's been a stressful couple of weeks. I know I should be happy I won. It just feels tainted, I guess."

The rest of the table is still silent. "Can we just focus on the crab legs and pie, maybe? For now, at least? I'll figure out how to enjoy my win. Eventually." Maybe, I add to myself.

"I second the moving on," Nik says. "I'm supposed to be the moody one. That's the musician's job, not the athlete's."

"Have you not seen football players after a game?" I look at Nik. "Talk about drama queens."

"That's usually agony over defeat. When they win, they're giddy. They're not complicated, you know."

"And you're complicated?"

Nik looks shocked, offended. "I am a deep and complex man, Kassandra."

"Deeply full of crap, maybe." I look at my parents just in time to catch them exchanging a smile. One of the many knots of tension loosens in my back. I have restored peace, convinced them everything is fine. I am fine. Nothing to be concerned about here. Just some normal teenage angst. I'm not sure how long I can keep up the charade, pretend doom dressed as a god doesn't lurk around every corner.

***

I need an escape from the eternal awkward that has become my life. I am starved for honesty, truth, surrounded by a sea of half-lies and deception. This makes my pending appointment with Apollo highly appealing. His danger is undisguised.

Once dinner is over and we are home, Nik claims the living room. He perches on an ottoman with his cello, lost in music. Hermione curls around Nik's feet, purring in sync with the notes pouring from the cello. Mom and Dad curl up together on the couch, each of them with a book.

I don't fit.

"I'm gonna take a walk," I say to the room. "It's been a day. I need to decompress a bit, I think." Conveniently my outburst at dinner makes this believable. I move to the door. "I might be gone a while, but I've got my phone."

"Watch for cars," Mom says, looking up for a moment. "I love you," drifts out before she dives back into her book. Dad's fingers sift absently through her hair.

I step out into the remnants of twilight and close the door behind me. This may not be a great idea. I am headed for a meeting with Apollo. In the dark. By myself. Everything about this is screaming bad idea. But I can't shake the hope he will fix what he has broken. Somehow. Plus, if I don't show, he will be pissed.

I imagine him arriving at my house. He would barge in, piling additional curses on me and my family. He might be armed with his golden bow. I'm not willing to risk them.

I walk along the side of the road, headed for the park and The Springs. This part of town is quiet and dark.

A single headlight comes at me. It swerves from one side of the lane to the other, the driver either drunk or just on the edge of control. The small engine putt-putts through the quiet night. It sounds familiar. It sounds like a moped. I smile. Joel.

He pulls to a stop beside me. "Kass. What're you doing?"

"I'm just going for a walk."

Joel nods. "Cool. I'm headed to your house. Wanna ride?" He tips his head to the back of the moped.

I shake my head. Even if I were headed home, I don't think I could make myself climb on his death mobile. "No thanks. I'll be back at the house in a while."

He nods again. "Hey. I heard you won today."

I give him a small smile. News of my flawed victory has traveled.

"Good work." We stand in silence for a moment. I feel like there is something more he wants to say. Or something I should ask.

"Wanna tell me who the girl is?"

"What?"

"You had that big mystery date a couple of weeks ago. You've managed not to mention it since." That either means it was a total disaster or the height of awesome. If it were a disaster, I'm pretty sure Joel would have told everyone about it. He would have made it into a funny story or a deep life lesson. My bet is on awesome.

He stares at me. "Nope. Not yet. Not time. I should get going."

"I'll see you later." I narrow my eyes and point at Joel. "There will be more questions."

His only response is to rev his little engine and scoot away.

I wait until he is out of sight, then turn onto the short drive to The Springs. There are no cars in the parking lot. No people in sight. I'm not sure if I beat Apollo here, or if he is already at the mineral pool, waiting. Plotting. I bite my lip. I wish I could turn around and go home.

I shake off the tension and push myself forward, down the path to the pool. With every step, I add a layer of steel to my spine, a layer of strength to face him.

He isn't here.

I step into the small clearing and move to the edge of the pool. I look out, past the line of palms and ferns to see the sliver of moon hanging over the ocean. I can't quite see the water, but I can hear the waves. The constant song of Delphi Springs.

I feel him behind me before he speaks. "Kassandra."

I turn to face him, take yet another deep breath and straighten my spine. The deep breath is a mistake. He is so close that his scent is all I draw in. No oxygen. Just the intoxicating mixture of wood, sea, and sun. A shiver ripples over me.

"Are you cold?" He nestles a water bottle by his feet and begins to unbutton his shirt. He clearly intends to strip off the plain white collared garment and give it to me. I wonder for a moment if it is possible that Apollo will be shot by his own arrow.

"No. I'm fine." There is no way I can handle his shirt on my skin, the smell of him wrapped around me. He continues unbuttoning, ignoring my words of protest. With every button, more of him is exposed to my view. This is the Apollo I first meet. He is all god again tonight. Apparently, he only dims his appearance for other mortals. I get the full show.

My hand shoots out and grasps one of his. "Really. I'm not cold." I jerk my hand back and wipe my palm on my jeans. It does nothing to remove him.

"So. What did you want to talk to me about?" I want him to say he thought of an addition to his curse that will undo the worst of the damage. If he can offer me that, I will try to negotiate something other than my virginity to compensate him.

"I want to offer you another chance." Apollo steps around me and settles on the large rock by the water.

"Another chance?" I'm not sure what these words mean. Another chance for him to fix things?

"Yes. Another chance to give me what I asked for." These are not the words I want.

"Is this a threat to make things worse if I don't change my mind?" So much for my thought he might try to make up for what he has done. That he cares at all about making things right.

"No. I thought I'd sweeten the deal, actually."

"Did you think of a way to add to the curse to make it better?"

"I can't take away your gift of sight. I can't give you a gift of persuasion or believability because that would directly contradict my second gift." He pauses for a moment. "I don't think there is anything I can do."

I look to the ground. I can't let him see the tears that spring to my eyes. I am going to be stuck forever with visions of events I will be powerless to change.

"I guess I should have thought the curse through before I kissed you." My eyes fly up. That would have been great, him thinking things through. "I should have realized the permanence of it, the ability to bargain that I was taking away." Apollo looks to the sky and chuckles. "I'm not really known for thinking things through." He drops his gaze back to me. "But there are other things I can give you. If you agree to give me what I asked for."

My teeth clench together to hold in the string of curses I want to throw at him. "I will be haunted. Forever." I push these words through the minuscule space I have allowed between my teeth. "I will see disaster after disaster. People I love hurt, maybe killed. I will know it is going to happen, know I can't do anything to stop it." I take a step towards Apollo. The trickle of words has surged to a tide. It has loosened both my tongue and my body. "And you still think you can get me to sleep with you as compensation for the gift you gave me, then broke?"

"I'm not looking for compensation for the gift. I'm aware that ship has sailed. And that it's my fault." He stops. His words settle over my skin. I feel them like the touch of his hand. He is a god. Admitting he made a mistake, caused a problem he can't fix. I soften.

"But I still want you," Apollo continued. "I still have things to offer you. I'm hoping we can make a deal."

"A deal for sex." I laugh. "So, to you, I am a prostitute."

Apollo stares at me, his brows furrowed. "I'm not offering to pay you."

"You're offering me more gifts. Or something else. In exchange for sex. Pretty sure that's the definition of prostitution."

"I'm trying to think of it as building a relationship. We both have things we want, things we can help each other get. That's a relationship."

"What do you have that I want?" I stand in front of him, my arms crossed tightly against my chest. He does have something I want. But I can't let myself have him.

Apollo reaches out and loosens my hand's grip on my left arm, forcing me to unfold. He places my right arm down at my side and focuses all his attention on my partial left arm. His fingers move over my stump. His touch sends tingles throughout my body. I watch his face. Any playfulness that had been there moments before is gone. He is a mixture of reverence and apology.

"I can heal you," he breathes. Apollo-tinged air flows over my skin, seeps into me. He does not look up at me.

I snatch my arm out of his hands. "I'm not broken."

"Kass, that's-"

"I don't need you to heal me," I cut him off. "I don't need fixing."

"I didn't say you were broken." Apollo rises, so close he towers over me. "It is partly my fault you lost your hand and part of your arm. Let me give it back to you."

"No." The answer flies fast, sharp.

He sighs and looks up at the sky, as if searching for guidance. "I haven't done anything right with you." I barely make out the whisper of words under his breath. His sadness and remorse blow away some of my anger.

He looks back down from the stars and catches my gaze in his own. He must see my uncertainty. He steps closer and leans down to tuck his nose and mouth close to my ear. His arms slide around my waist. "You are perfect. Perfection should last forever."

I want to pull him close and push him away at the same time. My eyes flicker to my arms to find I am doing exactly that. My stump is pressed in the center of his chest, pushing him away while my right hand is twisted in the fabric of his shirt, pulling him into me. If he weren't a god, if there weren't strings attached to every move I make with him, I would stop pushing. I would give in to what we both want.

"I can give you forever," he continues. His mouth brushes against the side of my neck. It makes it hard to hear him, process what he is saying.

What does that mean? I push harder with my stump, force my fingers to unfurl and release him from my grip. I push until there is enough space to meet his eyes. "What do you mean, you can give me forever? Do you want to marry me now?" The image of Apollo in a tux, walking down the aisle to meet me where I stand in a flowing white dress is both tempting and too much. I crack. Laughter bursts free like an arrow released from a bow.

"I wasn't thinking marriage, necessarily. But I guess I'm not ruling it out, either." Apollo's face is all business. "I meant I can give you immortality. You can live forever."

He is saying these very serious things, but I can't take any of them seriously. I continue giggling. "How would you do that?"

Apollo reaches down and lifts the water bottle he brought with him to the clearing. "All you need to do is drink this."

I squint at him and reach out to grab the bottle. I give it a gentle shake. I hear the slosh of liquid inside. "What's in this?"

"Nectar."

"Nectar." He does not offer further explanation. "Fruit juice is not going to make me immortal."

"It's not fruit juice. This is the nectar of the gods. This is what gives us immortality. If you drink it, a sip or two every day, you will also be immortal."

"Right." I no longer question my sanity, but this man is nuts.

"Kassandra, I'm serious. This is a rare gift. It has been bestowed upon very few mortals. You should feel honored. You are precious to me."

I narrow my eyes. "Your solution to the curse you kissed into me is to make me immortal. So I can live forever. Watching horrors I can't stop for, literally, the rest of eternity. Once again, you have found a way to make the situation worse." I shove the bottle back into his hands. "There is no way you are getting me to drink that."

I turn my back on Apollo and follow the path out of the clearing, leaving the mineral pool and the man behind. Such a waste of time. I stop before I am out of his sight and call over my shoulder, "and I am still not having sex with you." It's always best to be clear.

Chapter Thirteen

H alfway home, I hear the scuff of steps behind me on the road-side gravel. I spin, ready to either fend off an attacker or make a run for it. Of course it is Apollo. Of course he followed me. "What are you doing?" I ask. "I thought I was clear. I don't want what you have to offer." That's almost the truth.

"I'm making sure you get home safely. It's dark. There could be strangers lurking."

"None stranger than you," I mumble under my breath. I turn away and continue toward home and sanity.

"I heard that," Apollo calls.

"I don't care," I reply, in a sing-song voice. I know I am probably provoking more bad behavior from him, but I can't help it. I am tired of tiptoeing around him, around everyone. Tired of the effort to stay on his good side.

He follows me all the way to my driveway. My driveway. Home. I turn to stare him down, pushing down the bubble of panic pushing up from stomach. Now he knows where I live. I shouldn't have let him follow me.

Stupid. He is a god. He already knows where I live. He probably knows what I had for breakfast this morning, what color underwear

I am wearing. I shove my mind to safer territory. He probably knows Nik keeps a stash of chocolate hidden in his cello case.

This thought is not safer.

"You will not mess with my family," I whisper, my voice coiled tight. "You will not speak to my family. If you feel the need to spread around more agony and despair, pile it on me. But leave. Them. Alone." I bite back off the rest of my thought. No arrows near my family.

He smiles. "It's cute you think you have control over what I do or don't do."

"Please?"

"I'll consider it."

"Kass!" Julie's voice squeals behind me. I turn to watch her bound down the driveway. I glance over my shoulder. Apollo still stands near the curb. I can't be sure in the dim light from the streetlamps, but it looks like he has dimmed himself.

Julie crashes into me and wraps her arms around me. She turns us both around in a hoppy hug. As we turn, I see the front porch of my house. Is Joel's long hair swinging in the shadows?

"Congratulations!" Julies says, her voice more normal. "I'm so sorry I couldn't be there. Stupid job." She releases me and lets her hand slip down to catch mine. She gives me a tug, pulling my body toward the house.

One step later, she stops and looks behind me. "Who's this?" she asks. Julie leans in close to whisper in my ear. "He's gorgeous! Where did you find him?"

I wince and pinch my eyes shut. I know Apollo heard that. He heard everything Julie said. I can't just ignore him. I have failed to keep him separate from my family. He is here. He has been seen.

"Julie, this is Apollo. He's Coach Hamilton's new recruit."

"Oh," the single word is drawn out, almost a purr. "You're the guy who won today, right?" Julie flicks her hair over her shoulder.

"Of course," Apollo answers.

I roll my eyes.

Julie giggles and lays a hand on his arm. "At least you're modest."

Nope. "I should get in before Mom and Dad start to wonder if I'm ever coming home." The flirt-fest has got to stop. "Did I see Joel on the porch?" I try to draw Julie toward the house.

Julie looks at the porch, her eyes drifting over the front of the house. She shrugs, not meeting my eyes. "I think he's here. Probably inside with Nik." Julie turns her attention back to Apollo a little too quickly. "Do you want to come in for a while?"

"Julie!" I glare at her.

"What?"

I bite my tongue. I want to blurt he will only enter my house over my dead body. That kind of refusal would require a lot of explanation. I would have to spill it all. I have to go along with this; pretend he's not the worst thing that has ever happened to me. I hope there are enough people in the house to keep him from cornering me somewhere, alone.

Right now, Apollo seems subdued, quiet. Maybe he is truly sorry about the chaos he created for me.

Maybe he is just looking for his next opportunity to add more.

"Never mind." I blow out a sigh and lead the way to my door.

Joel is sprawled on the couch. One arm and one leg dangle off the front and brush the floor. Nik is still on the ottoman where I left him, his eyes closed, his face a dream as he sways with his cello. Our parents are nowhere in sight. They have no idea I just brought a vampire of sorts into our house.

Julie heads straight for the coach and smacks Joel's leg. "Make some room, slug."

Joel rolls to an almost upright position and tucks himself into the corner of the couch. I watch them for a moment. Julie hasn't looked at Nik since she walked through the door. After the burst of flirting with Apollo outside, she hasn't looked at him, either. Now she is next to Joel. Their heads are tilted toward each other as they talk quietly.

I look at Nik. His eyes are still closed. He hasn't acknowledged anyone is here. I'm not sure he noticed, actually. I turn.

Apollo is in the doorway behind me. His gaze is on Nik, following the movement of Nik's arm as it dances the bow back and forth across the strings. Apollo is mesmerized.

The world has shifted. Again. I would bet my bow Joel's mystery date was Julie. That they were on the porch, together, when I got home tonight. Now Apollo is entranced with Nik. I snap my fingers in front of Apollo's nose.

He twitches, then pulls his focus to me.

"What are you staring at?" I ask.

"He's beautiful," Apollo says. His eyes can't stay with me; they wander back to Nik. "Is that your brother?"

I hesitate, as if telling Apollo Nik's name will give him to Apollo. I feel like I am offering him up on a platter to a hungry god. If I don't, he'll just get the information he wants some other way. "Yes, that's Nik."

Apollo brushes past me. He moves into the room and sinks onto the edge of the couch next to Julie to watch Nik play. Julie diverts her attention away from Joel for just a moment. The smile on Julie's face tells me the words she speaks are playful, though I can't hear them. Apollo barely acknowledges Julie's overtures. He is intent on Nik's face.

I have been replaced in the eyes of a god.

I feel burning in my gut. It washes up my throat and forces my eyes to prickle with tears. I look through them, at my friends and enemy and try to put a name to the feeling that has overcome me. It is anger. It is jealousy. It is hurt. It is annoyance. It is confusion. It is everything, balled into a wad that makes me gag.

I cough. Once. Then again. I need to get this feeling, this mess, out. A string of gaspy coughs erupts, so violent Nik stops playing.

"Are you okay?" Nik asks as he stands and leans his cello against the ottoman, then moves to my side.

"I just," another cough interrupts my words. "Can't catch my breath." I can't get it out. I can't get him out.

Nik steers me to the armchair in the corner. He settles me into the seat and rubs my back. Julie moves to my other side and kneels on the floor next to me. I struggle to slow my breath. I struggle to purge the panic. I take in gulps of air. Some I immediately cough back out. Others stay with me long enough to give me valuable oxygen, long enough for me to regain my equilibrium. The coughs slow, then stop.

"I'm okay," I say when I have enough air to form words. I wipe away the tears that leaked from my eyes onto my cheeks.

"I'm going to get you some water." Nik abandons me, going to the kitchen.

I keep his red shirt in sight as he moves around the corner, then shift my gaze to the couch. Joel is still tucked into the corner. He watches me, as if he is assessing if he is needed. The rest of the couch is empty. I look around the room, searching for Apollo. I don't see him. I'm not sure that means he is gone.

"Where did Apollo go?" I ask Julie.

Julie pivots on her heels to take in the room, then shrugs. "I don't know. Do you think he left? Weird while you were choking. Or whatever that was."

I can only shrug. I can't explain what just happened. I can't explain all that has been dumped on me in the last few weeks. All that just collapsed on me like an avalanche.

"Very weird guy," Julie repeats. "Hot-cha-cha. But weird."

Nik is back, a glass of water in his hand. "Here you go."

I stare at the opening to the kitchen. I wait for Apollo to walk through. He doesn't. Maybe he really left. Maybe I don't have to worry about what he's up to. At least for now.

I am too tired to think about this mess anymore. I drink the water then head upstairs. I am half asleep before my head hits the pillow.

Chapter Fourteen

I am an ostrich. I can't deal with other humans. Or gods, for that matter. I hide for most of the day after regionals and everything that came after. I barricade myself in my room, sleep until I am exhausted again and try to pretend Apollo is not worming his way into every corner of my life.

Part of me wants to run to Nik and tell him everything. Spill it all at his feet so I can warn him of the danger of getting too close to the man/God that is clearly now interested in Nik. Nik will probably laugh at me, maybe call me crazy. He won't know how close to true crazy might be. If Apollo doesn't want Nik to know he is a god, there is no way I can prove it to Nik.

So, I tuck my head in the sand and hide from the chaos swirling around me.

I sneak down the stairs twice, inch into the kitchen without being seen smuggling food up to my room. On my second trip, there is a dinner plate waiting for me, tucked into the warm oven. Mom knows I need some time alone. I love her for giving me that gift. I hate myself for not thinking of her fingers earlier in the day.

I force my mind through trig homework and a response paper to Beloved for English. I fall asleep fantastically early, the lights in my room still blazing.

Monday morning brings the real world back into focus. School lurks, just a couple of hours away. I have no idea what it has in mind for me today.

I stare at the ceiling above my bed. I will have to interact with humans. And my long To Deal list.

Joel and Julie as a couple. That is going to take getting used to.

Nik might be bait for Apollo.

Apollo. The ongoing thorn in my side.

Visions I might not be able to do anything about.

Mom's finger.

A human in a white shirt.

Apollo's damn golden arrow.

I haven't even made it out of bed yet, and I am already on the edge of overwhelmed.

No choice but to tuck it all away. Move forward. Deal with the day and the list of problems. So, I do.

Julie walks through our front door at 7:30 on the dot, singing as she enters. I am already in the kitchen, my breakfast finished. Mom's fingers are all still intact. Nik drags himself to the island and the food it offers as Julie sweeps in.

"Good morning, Pitera clan! It's a lovely, sunshiny day out there. Don't forget your shades." Julie slides into the seat next to me. My view of the day does not agree with hers.

"You are extra chipper this morning," Mom says as she nudges a plate toward Julie.

Julie shakes her head and stops the plate. "Thanks, but I already ate. I've been up and ready to go for an hour already."

An alien has clearly taken over my perpetually late best friend. "Why are you so excited for a Monday morning?" I ask.

"I just know it's going to be a great day. It was a great weekend, and I know we're on a roll."

"Okay. I'm not sure a great weekend guarantees a great Monday, but I'll try to give it a chance." I turn to Nik. "You about ready?"

Nik nods and shoves the remaining half of a breakfast burrito from his plate into his mouth before he heads upstairs for his cello.

"That was disgusting," Mom says.

I nod. "You should see him in the cafeteria. Truly frightening. I'll see you this afternoon, Mom. Love you."

"Love you, Kass." Mom smiles at Julie. "Have a killer Monday."

Julie and I spend an awkward silent minute on the front porch waiting for Nik to strap his cello onto his scooter. I can't say the things I want to say.

"Sorry about Saturday night." I try to break the awkward, find our normal. "I know I kind of freaked out and then disappeared on you. It was a really long, overwhelming day at the end of a couple of nutty weeks."

Julie shakes off my apology. "No worries."

"Can I ask you something about Saturday?"

"Sure." Julie avoids eye contact, as if she knows what is coming and can't bear to watch it head for her.

"Were you with Joel?"

"You saw us both here." Well. That's almost an answer.

"That's not what I meant, Julie. You know what I meant. Before I got home."

Julie licks her lips and picks at the polish on her thumb. "Sort of."

"Sort of?"

"We were just talking. On the porch. Waiting for you. Or for Nik to be social. Ish."

"What about a couple of weeks ago? Joel told me he had a date but wouldn't tell me who. Was it you?"

Julie blushes, then caves. "Yes."

"Why are you guys being so secretive? It's awesome. I think." I really am excited for them, glad someone around me has a chance at a normal relationship. Unlike me and my most recent kissing partner.

"Honestly? It's just weird. Because of Nik."

I frown and lift an eyebrow. "What do you mean? You and Nik were never a thing. Or Nik and Joel."

"It's weird because I was so vocal about my sort-of obsession with him."

"Yeah, about that. Where did it go?"

"I don't know." Julie shrugs. "The second Joel asked me out, it just blew away. Like it was some sort of placeholder until the real thing came along, or something. I mean, I still appreciate his hotness, especially when he plays, but I don't want him for me anymore. I'm not sure I ever really did want him for me."

"You know Nik won't care, right? If he even notices you and Joel are together, he'll think it's fine."

Julie just nods, unconvinced. We both turn to see Nik roll his scooter-cello contraption out of the garage. "Wouldn't it just be easier to carry the cello?" Julie asks him.

"Maybe. But I built this. It's cool."

"It's a kids scooter with a bunch of bungee cords attached to it, Nik," I say.

"I know! Awesome, right?" Nik starts the roll to school.

***

More evidence of my tilted world waits for us on the sidewalk in front of our school. Joel stands alone, his body subtly bobbing to unheard music in his head. The second Julie sees him she runs and wraps her arms around him in a huge hug.

Nik turns his head to follow Julie as she blows past. "Wait. What?" he asks as he turns back to me.

I laugh. "Yep. She's over you."

"She was into me?"

"Never mind." I can't even begin to explain everything he has missed, so I leave him standing at the corner to catch up on his own.

I walk past the still hugging couple. It's weird to think of them that way. I pass the faux-Greek columns that line the front of the building and head for my locker.

"Hey, Kass! Congratulations! I heard it was close." I smile and wave at the herd of football players lurking in the atrium, but don't stop to talk with them. I see some white shirts in the herd. Apollo wouldn't shoot someone in school, right? I shake away the thought. I want to unload the mound of books from my back and put on the jacket stashed in my locker. The A/C seems to be on full blast this morning, despite the touch of fall in the air outside.

I spin the dial on my locker. The air is full around me, buzzing with the constant hum of chatter. Bright star bursts of laughter and shrieks of both delight and agony rupture the heavy air. Heavy wooden doors provide a bass drum back beat, while the lighter metal locker doors act as snares.

Yesterday's tater tots float through the halls, accompanied by the sharp tang of disinfectant and the gagging undertone of formaldehyde from the science labs.

The air is a cacophony of sounds, textures, smells. So thick I feel like I am swimming through it.

I resist the urge to step outside into the briny sea air. I imagine it startling my senses, replacing the cacophony with gentle elevator muzak. The smooth rolling waves would wash over me, broken only by the cawing of gulls and the occasional blare of an air horn.

Give me the music of the sea over the grating noise of school any day.

I have my jacket in my hand and am about to slip it over my head when I feel him. The hairs on my right arm are the first to sense him, all of them jump to attention as if drawn to him.

I slowly push my locker door closed to free my view. He is inches away. His hand turns the dial on the locker next to mine. What the hell? I can't speak, can't move. I can only stand still and stare.

He must feel the weight of me watching him, because he smiles. A hint of dimple appears in his left cheek. I haven't seen that before. Apollo turns, his smile widening, bright and gorgeous even though he is clearly in dimmed god mode. "What are the odds?"

I still can't speak. Every day he gets a little closer, more entwined with my life.

He speaks in my place. "Of me being assigned the locker right next to yours?"

I swallow, force my dry throat to move. "I think you might have manipulated those odds."

He chuckles. "You might be right."

"What are you doing here? What are you after now?"

"I'm a student here."

I glare. "You are in one of my classes. You are not a student. You're a god."

He shrugs. "Potato, potahto."

I want to hit him. Ball up my fist and send it sailing right into the gorgeous face. Bend the perfectly straight nose. Shatter those sculpted cheekbones. I bite my lip instead. Hard. So hard I taste the penny sharp snap of blood in my mouth.

"If you must know, I'm keeping an eye on you. And your brother. I'm invested in your fates."

I shake my head no, as if that will deny him access to me, to my life. To my brother. I know my denial is not enough to keep a god from sticking his nose wherever he wants. I would feel better if I knew what he was really after. It doesn't seem to be just me anymore. It is bigger than me. "If you're invested in my fate, why did you disappear Sunday when I was gasping for air? I could have died."

"You weren't dying. You were just panicking."

"I wasn't panicking."

"Kassandra. That was a panic attack. You just freaked out. You weren't in any danger."

"Why would I be freaked out?" I know exactly why I freaked out. But I need to know what Apollo knows, what he is thinking.

"Because I saw something else that I wanted."

Nik. "Something? That's a little harsh."

Apollo lifts one side of his mouth in a smirk. "I know you are freaked out I find your brother attractive. That's not my problem."

I grit my teeth. I have no comeback. Just anger and frustration.

"Speak of the devil." A wave of charm washes over Apollo's face.

My brows twitch together in confusion before I catch sight of Nik heading toward us. How did Apollo know he is walking this way? Apollo is looking at me, his back to Nik. "Leave him alone," I say. My words are mixture of demand, request, and plea.

Apollo is immune to all three. He smiles, then turns and leans his back against his new locker, his hands tucked into the pockets of his jeans. The movement gives me a moment to really look at him. Jeans. Ridiculous T-shirt with the high school mascot dancing across the front, Delphi High Sponges in Greek-stylized text above it. He looks casual. Relaxed. Not like a Greek god, just a high school god. Gorgeous, yes, but within the realm of possibility. He still looks dangerous to me. Dangerous to Nik. Nik won't have any idea who he is dealing with.

Nik walks up to me, so determined to get my attention that he doesn't notice the god lounging beside him.

I try to steer him away from Apollo, but the bulky cello in his hand makes it impossible to guide him through the narrow gaps in the hall's traffic. My eyes dart from Apollo to Nik. I watch for Apollo to lunge at Nik, as if he will reach out and take a bite, devouring my brother. Like the snakes on the path at The Springs could do to me. I am so distracted by Apollo's proximity to Nik that I don't hear anything Nik is saying.

"Hello? Did you hear me?"

"Sorry."

Nik follows my eyes as my eyes dart again. I can tell the moment he finally sees Apollo. A tiny spark blooms as Apollo stares openly back at Nik.

"Hi," Nik says. "Hey. You're the guy that won on Saturday! Congratulations, man." Nik shakes his head, admiration firing in his eyes. "A perfect score. I've never seen one of those. Kass'll never get one." Nik turns to me as he laughs at my expense.

I don't laugh with him. I watch Apollo watching Nik. The look on Apollo's face is the same one I saw before when he was looking at me. It is the look of obsession. Of desire. I realize now this is what I saw on his face Saturday night when he first saw Nik.

This time I can easily identify the emotion that bubbles up, trying once again to choke me. It is jealousy. It tastes green in the back of my throat. I know I should separate this god from my brother. I should keep Apollo from sinking his hooks into Nik, latching onto him the way he latched onto me.

The trouble is, I am still hooked.

I don't know how to extract myself, let alone my brother.

So, I close my locker and walk away. I leave them alone. Together.

They burn in the back of my mind. They flicker like a twisting candle flame, casting shadows over every other thought.

Chapter Fifteen

I am not surprised to find a god-man sitting in my living room when I get home from school. I didn't need a vision to know this was fated to happen.

Nik is on the ottoman, as usual, with Hermione curled on the chair behind him. Nik is playing my favorite piece. Something by Bach, I can never remember the name.

I stand just inside the door and close my eyes, letting the music wash over me. I pretend Nik and I are the only people in the room; Apollo isn't there, his eyes aren't all over my brother. I pretend Apollo doesn't exist, has never spoken to me, kissed me, cursed me. I pretend everything is back to normal. In my mind it is B.A. Before Apollo.

The piece ends, and Nik immediately launches into another. I open my eyes, leave my imaginary land of happiness. Apollo isn't watching Nik anymore. He is staring at me. I narrow my eyes, practice shooting death rays. What is his game? What does he want this time? Apollo doesn't die. He winks, then turns back to Nik and sinks into the deep cushions of the couch. God, I hate that wink.

I shake him off and head upstairs to finish my homework. Part of me hopes Apollo follows. If he is upstairs bothering me, he isn't in Nik's space, drawing him in. Apollo doesn't follow. I try to work on trig, but my mind has other plans. Images of what might be happening downstairs run across my homework.

Is Apollo talking to Nik right now, turning him somehow? Are they kissing? Ew. Not going there. Is Apollo dishing out another curse disguised as love or lust? Is he surrounding Nik with snakes? Giving him gifts? What if Apollo gives Nik foresight, like me? Could Nik handle that? Could he help me change the things I see?

I give up.

I slam my book closed and blow out a harsh sigh. I give myself over to my imagination, plop back on my bed, and close my eyes. The images of Nik and Apollo dance together, swirling and twirling until they become a blurred vortex and I slide into sleep.

The images scatter, leave my mind's eye clear to focus on a single image. This one is different than the rest. I am in it. Nik is not.

Apollo lounges on a low white marble bench, his naked torso long and lean, rippled with muscles. He leans, stretches out on the elbow that holds him propped partially up. A white linen garment I don't have a word for drapes across his hips, dips deep below his navel, reaching only to mid-thigh. The legs that extend from the linen are roped with thick coils of muscle, though they are relaxed now.

I sit on the ground in front of the bench, draped in white linen of my own. Mine is a toga that hangs from my right shoulder and extends to my ankles. My hair is intricately braided, woven with laurel leaves.

I have two full arms.

My left arm, the arm I don't think I miss, is stretched up to Apollo. My fingers sift through his curls.

I fall into my dream self, feel the silk of Apollo's hair against my fingers. I slowly spin one finger, twirl the curl around me, wrap myself in it. I swear the fingers in this not-real hand are more sensitive than the fingers in my real right hand. I reach up with both hands to test this, push through the curls at Apollo's temples, compare the texture.

Apollo smiles, lets his eyes drift closed. He is lost in the mini-massage I give his scalp. I tighten my grip on his hair, pull him closer. This is only a dream. I can do whatever I want. No repercussions.

I lift onto my knees to bring my face in line with his. When we are an inch apart, I stop. Wait.

He opens his eyes and stares into me. Apollo pivots, swings his feet onto the floor to move into a sitting position. I let go of his hair. My hands travel down his neck, his chest, to land at his waist. He is silk everywhere.

"Stand for me," he whispers.

I do as he commands; my knees unsteady when I gain my feet.

His hands fasten onto my own, our palms together, fingers interlocked. He leans into me, tugs me gently to him, pulls my lips to his. We breathe into each other, the kiss more than body meeting body.

He raises my left hand into the air, directing my attention to it. "It's good to be my immortal, is it not?"

I suck in a sharp breath. The quick movement of air pulls me back into my body, back into my room, back into reality.

I lay on my bed, taking quick gasps of air. Was that a dream? Or a vision? I still feel the silk of Apollo against my hands. Against my lips. It was so real. I have never had a vision while I was asleep, but I don't have a reason to think it couldn't happen. Everything I saw in the dream/vision was in line with what Apollo offered. My arm, returned. My life, unending. My lips paired with his. Forever.

I don't know if what I just saw was what I really wanted and was denying myself. Or if it was what I absolutely did not want, but was going to get anyway.

"Kass?" Mom's voice is accompanied by a gentle knock on my door. The door cracks open, and Mom peeks inside, squinting to see me in the dim room. "Did you fall asleep?"

"Yeah. I guess I'm still tired from the weekend."

"It was busy. And stressful. You'll catch up. Dinner is ready when you are."

"I'll be right there." I sit up on the edge of my bed and rub my eyes. I want to remove the image of the kiss, scrub it from my retinas. It doesn't work. The kiss hangs in front of me, the afterimage from looking at the sun.

Mom backs out of the door and closes it behind her.

I try to push away the dream, the feel of Apollo. I will see that kiss, feel his skin, over and over. I can only hope it is not a vision of the future. I hope it is at the same time.

I move to the door and head down to the kitchen. I can hear my family talking from halfway up the stairs but can't see them until I am nearly at the bottom. The first thing that comes into view is Apollo.

He is sitting in my spot. Next to Nik. Talking to our parents. Mom and Dad are smiling; laughter splashed across their faces. Apollo has charmed them, too. His tendrils weave deeper into my life with every passing moment. He is an inoperable tumor.

I step into the kitchen and move to an empty seat. I am on the opposite side of Nik from my usual perch. The change in perspective throws me. I look at Dad across the island instead of Mom. I see the left side of Nik's face instead of the right. The room is tilted, unstable. My whole world is.

Apollo greets me with a smile. He doesn't pause the story he is telling. I'm not sure if Nik or my parents see me. They are so enraptured in Apollo's tale that they don't even look my way. I try to follow his story, the comments tossed in by my family. It is impossible.

I keep seeing myself mid-kiss with Apollo. Superimposed over the kiss is Nik's hand. It touches Apollo's shoulder, his arm, his leg under our parents' line of sight. These images are real, now. Nik is into Apollo. He is acting on it. The look in Apollo's eyes mirrors Nik's. The attraction is mutual.

My parents are oblivious to the sparks in the room. They are enchanted by everything Apollo has to say. Apparently, he is an amusing man. I can't bring his words into focus. I hear only draggy, static-y slurs of sound. I smile and nod through dinner, build and unbuild cities in my mashed potatoes. No one notices I am there. Or that my mind is elsewhere.

I excuse myself when I can't take it anymore. My family lets me slip from the room, from their grasp. I'm not sure they notice my leaving.

The laughter and chatter from the kitchen follow me up the steps, dogging me until I close my bedroom door to block the sound.

I pace. My fingers work the air, clenching and unclenching, grappling with something I can't see. I am agitated. Annoyed. Homework is not happening.

I sit at my desk and pull open the bottom drawer. I lift out a plastic container, open it, and spill the contents across my desk. Clay. Tools.

I begin to form a body. I am making a cat. Or a horse. But then it stands up on two legs. Outlines of muscles appear on its torso, its legs, its arms. Curls begin to spring from its head.

I make a mini-Apollo. I stand him up in the center of my desk and stare at him. I hate him. I want to kiss him. I want to consume him.

I smash him flat.

The knob on my door shifts a second before the door opens. Nik barges in, his face the brightest star in the sky. He crosses the room and pushes aside my trig book and the papers scattered across my bed. He settles cross-legged and starts to say words I don't want to hear.

"Kass. He's amazing. Really amazing."

"I don't know if I can talk to you about this."

"I know. It's a little weird, 'cause I'm your brother and you probably don't want to hear about my love life. God knows I don't want to hear about yours." He shoots me a warning glance as if he expects me to start spewing info he doesn't want. Oh, if only he knew. "But you're my person for this kind of stuff. Joel can't hear it. He doesn't deal well with the details."

I nod; pretend it's the general thought of his love life that bugs me. He doesn't know it's really the specifics. Apollo. I can't give my brother advice without conflicting with my own interests. Or disinterests. But I can listen. I can use what Nik tells me to figure out what Apollo is up to. If he is truly into my brother or just using him as a pawn to manipulate me.

"Joel has never been a detail guy." I give Nik a sigh for show. "Go ahead. Spill. Tell me what happened." I manage a small smile on the outside. Inside I am braced to hear words that will cut me.

"I know I just met him today. I know I should be careful. He's basically a stranger, right? But Apollo is the first person I've ever been really attracted to. More than just acknowledging someone is cute, you know? I saw him and something inside me said 'Mine.' Like he belonged to me. Or I belonged to him." Nik pauses for a breath. "Do I sound crazy?"

"A little. But that's normal for you." I don't think he sounds crazy at all. I heard the same little voice inside myself when I met Apollo, too. I hear it every time I see him.

"I did something not normal. For me, anyway." Nik looks down at his hands, then takes a deep breath. He is preparing for something huge. He forces himself to look at me, forces himself to say the words.

I am terrified and intrigued. My brother stepping out of his shell would be a big deal. I just want it to be anyone but Apollo.

"I kissed him." The words come out in a gush, spraying me with acid. Nik is watching for a reaction, so I hide the burn.

"Of course you did." I feel like I am listening to myself from several weeks ago. How could anyone resist the draw of a god who wanted to kiss them?

Nik smiles. The fear falls from his face. "You don't think I made a mistake?"

"I didn't say that. It's too soon to tell what will come from the kiss, right? But I understand it had to be done. You had to kiss him. I get it." I almost ask if it was a good kiss. I know the answer, though. Kissing Apollo is an experience that lingers. I see it hanging over my brother still. Oddly, he seems to be coping with kissing a god better than I am. Perhaps because my kiss came with a curse. Maybe just because I know he is a god.

Nik's smile widens. "I think I'm gonna get out of here. There is probably a limit to what I can share with my sister. I'm not sure where that line is, and it'll be really gross and awkward if I barrel across it." Nik pauses for a moment, debating saying more. "Yeah. Stopping there. Good night, Kass." He leans over and plops a kiss on my forehead, then leaves my room.

I rub at the tainted kiss on my forehead. I know where his lips have been. The innocent kiss feels heavy on my skin.

I lay back and stare up at the ceiling. The glow-in-the-dark stars I placed there several years ago peer down at me. I pretend I am looking up at the real night sky, maybe looking up at Apollo. At this moment, I would give anything for a vision. One glimpse of the future that would help me figure out what I should do. Should I be worried about Apollo and my brother? Should I let them be, let Nik be happy? Should I try to win Apollo over to me? Should I be doing everything in my power to make Apollo disappear, for good this time?

It's enough to make the stars spin.

Chapter Sixteen

Sleep refuses to be caught. Apollo and Nik, Julie and Joel rampage through my thoughts, keep my brain from shutting down. I am unable to let the day go. I give up long before dawn. I am left restless. Cranky.

I change from my unhelpful pajamas into sweats and long-sleeved t-shirt, and lace on a pair of shoes. Stealth slides with me down the stairs, dodges the creaky bottom step Dad keeps forgetting to reset. Hermione and Luna dart in and out of my legs. They don't understand why I am walking around the house while it is still so dark, but they are in for any adventures that are to be had. Nighttime navigation with two cats underfoot almost sends me sprawling on the floor. I make it to the kitchen, then out the back door and to the path to the beach. A walk on the sand will clear my head, chase away the swirling mess.

The moon is up, close enough to full to light my way. The sand glows under the clean white light. Waves roll gently onto shore. Moonlight dances and skitters across them, a spill of diamonds. I drop to my knees in the soft sand, then shift to remove my shoes. My toes naked and unafraid, burrow deep into the sand. The warmth trapped underground from yesterday's sun seeps into me, heating my toes.

I sit with my arms wrapped around my knees. The waves and moonlight dance together, serenaded by the music of the sea. Without touching me, the water washes away the jumble of thoughts in my head, leaves my mind clear.

As if a clear mind is the trigger, the vision strikes.

Nik stands before me, his face confused, almost angry. An arrow sails toward him, then lodges in his chest, sinks deep. The arrow shaft buried in his flesh is solid gold, with white feather fletching. Nik's hands move toward the arrow, hover over the shaft, not willing to grab hold. Nik falls to the ground; the white of his shirt marked with a growing blood-red circle around the arrow. I fall to my knees next to Nik and am powerless to help him. I can only watch the tendons of his neck strain with the effort to pull in air.

I gasp for my own breath back on the beach. My hands grasp at my chest as if they expect to find an arrow there. I pull the cool salt breeze deep into my lungs, struggle for any oxygen I can gather.

This time I have no doubt what I saw was a vision. An event fated to happen. My brother is going to be shot by one of Apollo's golden arrows. He is going to die. He is the person in the white shirt.

Unless I stop it.

Tears slip down my face. I am the only person who can stop it. But no one believes me. No one takes my warnings seriously, or listens to them at all. How can I keep Apollo from shooting Nik when Apollo is the very person who cursed me in the first place?

Apollo's curse already distorted my power. Now it will take away my brother. I rise to my feet and stumble forward. My feet sink deep into the wave-soaked sand as I cross the tide line. I keep walking, out into the water. I don't stop until the waves touch my shoulders.

I stand in the ocean and let the waves lift me. My salty tears continue their journey down my face until they unite with the sea. I tip back, let myself float on the surface. I look up at the moon, at the stars.

"I hate you," I say to the sky.

I float. I am lost.

I don't have time to be lost.

I right myself and wade back to shore.

He is there, as if he heard me call him, dressed only in the linen from my dream. This is the Apollo I first met. The Apollo who is too gorgeous to believe. All cut muscle, tan skin, blond curls, and eyes like the sea at dawn. He takes my breath. He rips out my insides and wads them up into a jumbled ball then shoves them, writhing, back inside me.

He stands tall, watches me as I move through the water, waits for me to reach his side.

My clothes are soaked, and the pre-dawn air is cool. I shiver as I emerge from the sea and the air touches me, sucks out what little warmth I have. Walking into the ocean fully dressed may not have been my best idea.

Apollo lifts a hand to my shiver, passes it through the air in front of me. I feel a puff of warm, dry air, as if Apollo has opened an oven door in front of me. I look down. My clothes are dry. I shiver again, this time not from cold. His implied touch makes me tremble.

"Thanks," I mutter. I don't allow myself to meet his eyes.

I stand a few feet in front of Apollo for a full minute, looking at my toes. I feel Apollo watching me, waiting for me to speak. My toes remain fascinating. I watch them push the sand back and forth.

"You had something to say?" he finally prompts.

I wonder if he watches me all the time, listens to everything I say, if he can hear my thoughts. Did he hear my conversation with Nik last night, laced with evasion and half-truths? Did he hear the words I didn't say to Nik? Or did he just hear me today because my words were so heavy with venom?

"I think you heard me." I still don't meet his eyes. I do venture my gaze from my feet over to his. Even his toes are gorgeous. Strong, not gnarled, tan, and pedicured. Hmm. His perfection is annoying.

"I did." He pauses. He wants me to speak, explain myself. Defend myself. As if I can.

I remain silent.

"I have a feeling there is more you need to say. I'd like to hear it." His perfect toes move closer to mine, closing the distance between us. A smile twitches across my lips. Funny he thinks he can bridge the chasm between us. He is the man who will kill my brother. That forms an uncrossable void.

As he inches closer, more of him moves into my view. His calves, sprinkled with blond hair. His knees. Knees always look awkward, bumpy. His look like rolling hills of delight. The edge of his linen skirt-thing swings into view as he stops. I trail my eyes upward, move over the carved lines of his stomach and chest to find his face. I bite my lip, both to hold in the string of curses I want to unleash and to keep from licking my lips. He might interpret that as an invitation to swoop in for a kiss.

That might be exactly what it is. I can't sort out the hate, the fear, the longing. They swirl together in my chest.

Apparently biting my lip is just as inviting. Apollo sucks in a sharp breath. I watch his eyes shift, dilate, as he reaches out a hand to me.

I take a step back. "Nik." I spit the name at him. I want him to know I know where his lips have been, who he has been kissing. When he's not kissing me. Saying my brother's name brings on a fresh bout of tears.

The hand that was destined to wrap behind my neck and pull me in for a kiss changes course. It moves instead to my cheek to catch the tears and wipe them away.

"What's wrong?" Apollo asks. "Why are you crying?"

I have no idea where to start. Should I start with the problem Apollo knows about, the one he caused with his kiss? Or the problem my visions showed me? I close my eyes and try to see a path through this mess. One that ends with Nik and me both alive and preferably not miserable.

With my eyes still closed, I feel Apollo's fingers land on my face. He wipes away the fresh layer of tears, then traces the contours as if he is trying to see me through his hands.

"Kass. I can't even try to fix things if you won't talk to me. Tell me why you're angry. And sad." His voice is soft, a gentle caress that steals into me.

"I want you to tell me what you want." I open my eyes. I need to read the truth on his face.

Apollo chuckles. "Well. I want you."

"And how does kissing Nik, wooing him, get you that?"

"I didn't say you were all I wanted."

"What else?"

"I want your brother."

I shake my head. How can he not understand the immense conflict captured in his tiny list of wants? I want to understand his logic, if there is any, so I try another question. "Why do you want us?'

He smiles. "At first, I wanted you because you owed me something. Something it would be my pleasure to take. But then I really saw you. You are fierce, Kassandra. Perfect in your tenacity, your will."

"Then why kiss Nik?"

"I want what I want. Nik is what I want."

"I don't understand how you can claim to want us both. I don't work that way. What I want is exclusive to wanting other things. Other people." I want Apollo to think I am jealous; I want to keep him for myself. Maybe that will keep him away from my brother. I will do anything to keep that arrow from piercing into Nik. "You offered me nectar, offered to make me immortal. That would chain me to you for eternity." I soften my voice as I meet Apollo's eyes. "I thought you wanted me for eternity."

"I do, Kassandra. I earned the right to have you once with the gift I gave you. Watching you resist me, watching you take on the world, has made me want to keep you forever."

I'm not sure what to do with those words. They are far from a declaration of love and devotion. "Am I a trophy to you? A prize? Or do you love me?" The last question is a whisper. I want to pull it back the second it drifts from my lips.

I want him to love me. I want to know I am valued in his eyes. Yet the thought of his love terrifies me. A god in love will do anything, destroy anything in his path, to get what he wants.

"You are one in a million, Kassandra." Apollo steps closer. His hands brush up my arms to cup my shoulders and pull me into a hug. I let myself fall into him. "I want you near me, always. I want to watch you take on the world. I want to give you everything to make you happy." He pauses. His arms slide down my back to wrap around my waist. I am captured. I don't care. I nestle my head into his bare chest. I can hear the steady beating of his heart. It surprises me, that a god has a heart, like a normal human. I am so entranced by the metronomic rhythm that I almost miss his next words. "I don't love you. At least not the way you mean. I certainly find you attractive. I am drawn to you. I would welcome you as part of my future." He trails off, lost in his own thoughts.

I am tumbling again. Why does he continue to pursue me, woo me, if he doesn't really love me? I am just something for him to obtain. A goal to conquer. I slip my arms between us and push hard on his chest. He releases me. Too easily.

"What about Nik?" I ask. I don't want to hear this answer, either.

A sweet smile spreads on Apollo's face. "Nik. Nik is indescribable. He plays for me. I feel it in my bones. He has burrowed inside me with that cello of his. When I saw Nik, it became clear to me that what I feel for you is want. Desire. It is strong, it drives me, but it is not love."

I watch his face bloom as he talks about my brother. The look is not the lusty craving he displays when he talks about me. It is pure. "You love him." It is a statement to myself, as much as to Apollo.

He stills for a moment, then nods. "Perhaps I do."

I continue backing away. I shake my head with each step, as if I can deny his words, make them go away. Make him go away.

"Kassandra, my love for Nik doesn't change anything."

"I think it changes everything." I want to yell the words, launch them at him like arrows. But they slice me too much. I have to ease them gently out of my mouth and into the air.

Apollo's face twists into a question mark, his brow furrows, mouth open slightly in confusion. "What do you mean?"

I take a deep breath. I want to tell him. Describe my visions, the sight of the arrow from his bow piercing Nik, spilling his blood. Killing him. I want to hurt him with the words, the truth of what he is going to do to the person he claims to love. But I have been cursed. By Apollo himself. No one believes my warnings. Does that apply to the gods as well? Will Apollo believe me if I tell him what he will do to Nik?

"Your relationship with him is dangerous," I finally blurt.

"For who?"

"For all of us." This is the truth. Nik will die. I will lose my brother, the other half of my soul. Apollo will lose his love.

"I don't understand. What is the risk?"

I gnaw on my lip, hesitant. The only possible way to get through this is to just go for it. "You are going to kill him."

The words have been festering, painful inside me. They don't feel any better on the outside. They hang heavy in the air, drown out even the sound of the waves behind me.

Apollo takes a single step in my direction. "That is ridiculous. If you think I'm going to break his heart, I can promise I won't. Even if I do, a broken heart never killed anyone."

"No. You are literally going to kill him. With one of your stupid golden arrows. I watched it sink into his chest. I saw the blood pour out. I saw him die."

"I would never do that. I would never shoot him or put him into a situation where he was in danger."

"You will. I saw it. Visions, remember?" Even with the curse, I can't believe Apollo doesn't believe me, that he doesn't see the risk. "Your 'gift' to me?"

Apollo nods.

I have a moment of swelling hope. He knows I have visions of the future. That's more than anyone else knows. He will heed my warning, he has to. "I had a vision. Here. Just before you showed up. I saw Nik, shot by one of your arrows."

"It's not going to happen, Kassandra. Not all of your visions come true, right?"

This stops me. Technically, he's right. When I intervene, when people listen to me, do what I push them to do, things go differently than they did in my visions. Technical truth and practical truth are not the same. I slowly shake my head. "Sometimes I am able to change things."

"How do you know you changed anything? Maybe events wouldn't have happened as they did in your vision, even without your interference."

That would mean they are delusions, hallucinations. It would mean I don't have a gift at all. I am crazy. I've been down this road before. "When I don't act, bad things happen. When people don't listen, bad things happen." I am desperate for Apollo to listen, to hear me and take my warning to heart. Pleading oozes from my words, from my pores.

I move toward him, try to snare him in my sincerity. I place my hand on his arm and lean close, hoping the contact will help the truth soak in. "Please, listen. I know you think you would never hurt him because you love him." I choke a little on these words but manage to push through. "But you will. I don't know how you will get to that point, what will lead up to it, but it will happen. You will shoot Nik." I give the words a chance to settle in, burrow under his skin. Fester.

"If you want to save him, leave him alone. Stay away. From him. From me." My heart pounds. Adrenaline rushes through me, nerves sizzling. I feel as if the arrow is flying through the air now, this moment my only chance to stop it.

"I believe you want me to stay away from Nik. But I don't think it's because I will hurt him. I think you want me all to yourself." Apollo brushes his finger over my cheek. "This really is beneath you, Kassandra. You are better than this. And you can't keep me away from him."

Apollo leans forward and places a gentle kiss on my cheek. He is gone before the sharp of his words pierces me.

I spin. I want to find him standing behind me, or down the beach.

I am alone. Even the moon has abandoned me.

I drop to my knees in the sand and close my eyes. I try to re-see everything my vision showed me. I need to catch every detail. Every clue gives me a chance to see when, or where, the awful is going to happen. There is nothing. The vision stayed so tight to Nik, to the blood staining his white shirt, that all context was stripped from the event, as if it would happen in an abyss all its own. I can't even be certain Apollo was the one who sent the golden arrow flying.

Today's vision added more detail to the previous one. Maybe I will have another vision, one that gives me enough information to save Nik.

But how can I stop what I see? No one believes my warnings. I don't have enough information. I will have to be so vague that everyone will think I am crazy. Or I'm just jealous.

They might be right on all counts.

I am crumpled on the sand when the sun slips over the horizon. Light washes over me but does nothing to illuminate the inside. I stand and scrub the salt from my face.

My only option is to keep Apollo and Nik apart.

Somehow.

Chapter Seventeen

I stumble through the day. I put on a mask, a smiling face that shows everyone around me my world is not falling apart. No one tries to peek beneath, see the chaos and confusion that lies below. Knowledge sits heavy on my shoulders, rolls them in, shuts out everyone around me. I build up a protective shell and carry the weight alone.

Knowing who is going to be shot by Apollo's arrow is so much worse than not knowing. I want my ignorance back.

By the time the last bell rings, I am wiped. No sleep and the fear of failure, of losing Nik, makes me want to curl up on my bed, pull the covers over my head and sleep for two days straight. I want to shut out everything that has happened, everything that will happen. That is not an option. I don't know how much time I have to save Nik. The arrow could find his chest at any moment. Today. Tomorrow. Next week. I might not see it coming, not until it is too late to stop the arrow, change its path. I need to fix it. Now.

Telling Apollo what he was fated to do did nothing to convince him to stay away from Nik. I could try the opposite approach, warn Nik. The problem is how much to tell him. He doesn't know I have visions. If I tell him now, he might not believe any of it. He might think I am jealous, I don't want him to have a relationship, with anyone. Even if he does believe me about the visions themselves, I still have to overcome the freaking curse.

The curse is a large enough obstacle on its own. I'll leave the whole vision-thing out, for now, at least. My best bet is to convince Nik his relationship with Apollo isn't in his best interests. Convince him he shouldn't fall for the gorgeous, seemingly perfect man. I will have to break my brother's heart to save his life, make him doubt the relationship that makes him the happiest I have ever seen him. I will have to make him hate me as much as I want him to hate the god that threatens him.

I beat Nik home. Mom and Dad aren't here yet. That helps. This is not a conversation I want to have with a parental audience. I hope Apollo doesn't walk home with Nik. If Apollo does show up, I will have to find a way to make him go away. That's going to be difficult. He is an immovable object. Apollo will see what I am doing in a heartbeat. He'll know I am trying to split them up.

I nestle into the porch swing and prop my feet up on one of the columns that line the front of our house. I don't have to wait long. Nik walks alone, pushing his weird scooter-thing beside him. I let out a breath. One obstacle gone.

"Hey," I say as Nik rolls up the driveway. "Got a few minutes? I need to talk to you."

"I was going to practice."

I stare at him.

He gets the message.

"I guess it can wait. What's up?"

I grab Nik's hand and pull him down on the swing beside me. I turn sideways and tuck my feet underneath me so I can face him. My nervous hand drifts to my hair and finds a stray curl to twist.

"Kass?" Nik pokes my thigh. "What?"

I start with the only completely honest thing I may say during this conversation. "There's something I'm worried about."

Nik makes a spooling gesture, urging me to get on with it.

"I'm worried about Apollo. About your relationship with him."

Nik stays calmer than I expected. I thought I would get automatic defensive outrage. Instead, he drops back into the corner of the swing and shows only a flicker of anger on his face. "Seriously?"

"I'm worried you're going to get hurt." More truth. Partially. I mean a different hurt than Nik thinks. "This is your first relationship. I don't want you to get too attached, too fast."

"Kass. I'll be fine. Apollo and I are good." The twinge of anger flees Nik's face. It is replaced with peaceful bliss.

He is in deeper than I realized.

"He just seems more... experienced, I guess. I worry you two aren't in the same place, that you aren't moving at the same pace, and might not always be in sync. That could end badly for you." Plus, he's a god. With golden arrows of death.

The right side of Nik's mouth quirks up in a wicked grin. "We're in sync. Trust me."

"Ew. I don't want to know what you mean by that."

Nik laughs.

I nudge him with my knee. "Are you sure he's as into you as you are into him?" I don't really want to go down this road. But it might be the only thing that can pry these two apart.

"Yeah. He is."

"Are you sure?"

"Why are you asking that? Why would I doubt it? Why would I doubt him?"

I dodge the true answers with questions of my own. "He hasn't been here long. Do you know anything about his past? Does he have a boyfriend where he came from? Another boyfriend here? A girl-friend?"

"He's not seeing anyone else. I would know."

"Would you?"

Silence falls on the swing.

I break it. "I don't think he's who he says he is. I think he's showing you a facade, there's someone else hiding inside. I mean, how well do you really know him? He could be keeping all kinds of secrets."

Nik is up and off the swing. His sudden movement sends me swinging so hard I have to grab the swing and kick my legs free to keep from falling off. Nik takes several steps away, then turns back to look at me.

"What do you think he's keeping from me?"

There are so many answers to the question that I almost forget what Nik already knows. What he doesn't know. I take a moment to re-orient myself to the context of his question.

"You're not the only person he's into." I dodge. I don't want to confess my odd relationship with Apollo.

"What? What do you know?"

"He kissed someone else. Like a few weeks ago, when he first got here. Before he met you. But I think he's still into her. Sort of."

"Her?" Nik looks puzzled. And hurt.

I hate that I am causing him doubt, causing him pain. It hurts me. But I need to make it worse. I need to make it so awful, so painful, that Nik never wants to see Apollo again. I have to make him bleed. I start with a nod.

"Who?" Nik asks. "Do you know? Is it someone I know?"

I nod again and look down at my hand. My grip on the edge of the swing is so tight that my knuckles are white.

"Who?"

I am silent. These words will cut both of us.

"Kass, you have to tell me."

I close my eyes. I can't watch the damage. "Me."

The porch is silent and still. For a moment, I can hear only the jagged movement of my own breath, the smooth rolling of waves in the background. Then I hear the slap of shoes against the pavement. I open my eyes to see Nik's back as he stalks away from me. He grabs his cello and turns into the garage.

He is angry. Hurt. That's what I wanted. What I needed. I just wish it didn't hurt me so much. I can only hope Nik's anger isn't just for me. He needs to hate Apollo, avoid him, never speak to him again. The anger needs to keep Nik out of the arrow's path, forcing him to avoid his fate.

Inside the garage, the door to the house slams. I wince. I might have saved my brother only to lose him. I wait.

I can't.

I stand to head inside, find Nik and try to apologize. Maybe I can steer all his anger toward Apollo. Before I can take a step, the wail of Nik's cello wraps around me. I turn to look through the window behind the porch swing. Again, I am looking at Nik's back. He is curved over and around his instrument, as if he is hugging it.

The music is not like a hug. It is harsh. Fast. Angry. It is a person yelling, venting anger and frustration. This is nothing I have heard Nik play before. He tends toward the mellow. Gentle. Seductive. This is a scream.

I move around the swing to stand at the window. I lay my palm flat against the glass, my hand superimposed over his bent form. I pretend I am touching him.

"Please don't die."

Chapter Eighteen

"**W**hat are you doing?"

I spin away from Nik's tortured image to find Julie standing at the foot of the porch steps, her face twisted in confused concern.

"Nothing. Just watching Nik play." I try to push my lips into a smile, but they resist.

"Why'd you disappear so fast after school? I turned around and you were gone."

"I'm really tired. I just wanted to get home and relax."

Julie's eyebrows lift. "And here you are, staring through the window at your brother. That's not weird at all, Kass."

My lips are more cooperative this time. The smile almost makes it to my eyes. "Sorry. I know I've been... odd. I've had a lot on my mind."

"Like what?"

This is a perfectly reasonable question from my best friend. I want to sit down and tell Julie everything. Apollo's gift. The kiss. The curse. The visions. Spill it all out into the open, let Julie sop up the mess. Why shouldn't I? Julie will either believe me, or she won't. I might be able to convince her to help me split up Apollo and Nik.

Worth a try. But I can't do it with Nik lurking on the other side of a thin piece of glass. "It's a long story. Beach?"

Julie rolls her eyes. She is not a fan of the beach. She hates the feel of ocean water on her skin; claims it instantly dries her out. She knows how much I love it, so sometimes I manage to drag her along.

"Fine." Julie gives me a huge sigh so I can appreciate what a monstrous sacrifice she is making for me.

Julie trails behind me down the path to the beach. We are quiet. Except for the occasional sigh from Julie. I stop well back from the water line. If the water gets too close, threatens to come within a ten-foot radius of Julie, we will have to move.

I nestle down into the dry sand. Julie sits beside me, then dramatically brushes away a few grains of sand that cling to her hand where she braced herself on the way to the ground.

"All right, girl. Spill. I know you have a story to tell."

"Once upon a time..."

A glare silences me.

"Fine. It's all about Apollo."

"Wait. That obscenely hot guy Nik is into? Really?" Julie switches from pained to perky. I have captured her interest. "What happened?"

"He showed up on our sixteenth birthday. At The Springs."

"What?" Julie looks surprised and a little hurt the story has been brewing for several weeks and I haven't shared it with her.

"After you and everyone else had left. I stayed behind because I wanted some time alone. Apollo showed up and told me a lot of things. Things that are a little hard to believe, but that are all true."

Julie gives a small nod. Her head says she is with me, but the hurt on her face disagrees. I kept a secret. Taboo with best friends. This is going to get worse. I have kept a lot of secrets.

"First, he's not quite who he appears to be."

"Really. Who is he?" Julie's voice is hesitant, but curiosity and disbelief trickle under the surface.

I lick my lips and swallow. This might be the hardest bit for Julie to accept. If she believes this, the rest might be easy by comparison. "He's the actual god. Apollo."

"No way." Julie snorts and rolls her eyes. "I thought you were going to tell me what's been bugging you, not tell me a fairy tale."

"Myth. Not fairy tale. And it's true. He is really *the* Apollo. He's been showing everyone a muted form of himself. Well, not me. I've seen him full-out. You think he's amazing, but you haven't seen him at full strength. He's beyond.... Everything." I gaze out over the water. The last time I was here Apollo had given evidence of his godliness yet again, instantly drying my clothes. He had also refused to believe me, believe my vision. That was only this morning. It feels like a lifetime ago.

"Are you serious?" Julie finally asks. I shift my attention back to her.

"You really think he's a god." She isn't asking. This is a statement. She must see on my face that I believe.

"He is. He proved it. Several times. The first time, on my birthday, he sliced my arm open, then he healed it while I watched." I hold out my arm for Julie to inspect. "Look. No scar."

Julie turns my arm back and forth. "If you say so."

I know what she is thinking. There was never a cut at all, so of course, there is no scar. How can I convince her what I am saying is true?

"He also explained something that's been happening to me. Something I haven't told you about. Something that makes it sound like I've lost touch with reality."

"Weellll..." Julie stretches the word out, refusing to confirm my sanity.

My only defense is to blurt. "I've been having visions. Visions of things that are going to happen. Things I can change, stop from happening."

"Kass. That's not possible." Julie's voice is soft as her hand reaches out and settles on my arm. She is sympathetic, placating. She doesn't believe me.

"You remember that car accident? The one that totaled Steve's car?" I ask.

"Yeah. What about it?"

"Do you remember how you were planning to get home that day?"

Julie is silent for a moment. "I was going to ride with Steve. We were dating then. He always drove me home."

"Why didn't you?"

Julie looks away. Her eyes point toward the ocean, but I don't think she sees the water. She is probably seeing the halls of school instead. "You asked me to help you make a banner, right?"

I nod. "I had a vision that morning. You were in the car with Steve when he was hit. The other car hit the passenger door, mangling the whole side. In my vision, you were in the front passenger seat. I couldn't really tell if you were hurt, or if Steve was. But there was blood."

"Oh, my god."

"I made up a reason to keep you at school, keep you out of his car." I skim my eyes over Julie's face. The rich tan of her skin is unusually pale. "You weren't in that accident because I saw it coming. Because I pulled you out of it."

"Oh, my god," Julie repeats. "I was supposed to be in the car." Her eyes flit around, then land on me. "This is like those stories where someone says they just knew they shouldn't get on the plane and then the plane crashes and everyone dies."

Julie pops to her feet and begins to pace. She is so distracted she steps over the water line. A wave licks her foot, soaks her sandal. She doesn't notice the touch of salt water against her skin. "Oh, my god, Kass. You're psychic!"

Julie's pacing comes to an abrupt halt. "Wait. What does this have to do with Apollo? Did you see him coming or something?"

"That's what I'm about to get to."

"Okay. Tell me."

"When Nik and I were little, I was bit by a snake. You know that part."

Julie plops back onto the sand in front of me. She is still oblivious to her wet foot and now the sand sticking to her bare legs and hands.

"Apparently Apollo sent the snake. He sent a bunch, actually. Nik and I were all twisted up with them. One of them licked my ear." I pause. "That's even weirder out loud than it sounded in my head."

"Ew. Super gross."

"Yeah. But that lick gave me a gift from Apollo. He gave me visions, the ability to see things that haven't happened yet. The snake also bit me, though. That wasn't part of Apollo's plan. At least that's what he claims."

"A gift by snake lick. Kass, do you know how weird this sounds?"

"That's why I didn't tell you. Or anyone else. I sound like a lunatic."

"So, that's it? You can see things? Before they happen."

"That's not the end of the story. I wish it was. Apollo came back on our birthday this year because he wanted something in exchange for the gift he gave me."

"Interesting. What did he want?"

"He wanted me to have sex with him."

"No. Way." Julie leans in close. "Did you do it?"

"No!" I shove her away. "I refused."

"Why? If a guy that looked that good wanted to sleep with me, I don't think I'd be able to turn him down. He is hot."

"I don't love him. I don't even know him. He's a god. It seemed like a door I didn't want to open. I mean, what would he ask for next if I agreed to sleep with him once?"

"Hmm."

I can tell Julie doesn't agree with my decision.

"I did kiss him, though."

"You kissed that gorgeous piece of man and didn't tell me? Kass. I swear."

"It was a huge mistake."

"How could kissing him be a mistake? He is gorgeous. He oozes sexy. I'm sure the kiss was amazing. All smolder and smoke."

I feel the blush creeping up my neck. I remember exactly how amazing the kiss was, how lost I was in it. In him. "It was amazing. And awful."

"What?"

"With the kiss, he gave me a curse. He made it so no one believes my warnings about what I see in the visions. I can't do anything to change or stop what I see."

"Oooh, that's mean."

"Yeah."

"So, you can see awful things that are about to happen. But you can't do anything about it."

That sums it up. "I saw Shannon get hurt before it happened. I warned her to tighten her release. She didn't listen to me. She insisted it was fine."

"Holy crap."

"He didn't stop there. The curse wasn't the end. He keeps asking me, trying to persuade me to have sex with him. As if I would even consider it now that he's cursed me. Now that he's with Nik." I pretend I'm not still tempted. "He even offered to fix my arm."

"Seriously?"

"Yep."

Julie pulls her cheek between her teeth and worries it while she thinks for a minute. "Did you consider it?" she asks.

"No. Why would I?"

"Well. Having both arms. That could be good." Julie's voice is hesitant. She feels her way through the words as she says them, not sure if she agrees with herself or not.

"I wouldn't be me," I say. "I wouldn't know what to do with that arm, a strange thing stuck onto me." My dream, or what I hoped was just a dream, flickers through my mind, through my body. I shift my fingers where they rest on my leg, feel the silk of Apollo's hair instead of my own skin. I can think of one thing I would do with the arm. I shake my head. "No, thanks."

"Did he offer anything else?"

"A drink."

"A drink?" Julie quirks up one eyebrow.

"Of nectar. He offered me immortality. He wants me to go live with him forever or something."

"And you don't think he loves you?"

"He doesn't." My voice is far more confident in this statement than the rest of me. "He admires me, desires me. But like a possession, something he would be proud to own. Not like a partner. Not like he wants Nik."

"Whoa. You think he loves Nik?"

"More than he loves me, at least."

"Hmm."

"What?" I ask. Julie has the look she only gets when she is hatching a plan that will wander right along the edge of bad idea land.

"What if you did?"

"What if I did what?" I have not followed her into bad idea land.

"Sleep with him. Would it fix anything?"

Ah, her bad idea land is right next door to my land of temptation. "Probably not. He can't take back the curse. He told me once a god gives a mortal a gift, or a curse, it's there. Forever. No take-backsies. So even if I give him what he wants, he can't fix what he has already broken." I stop talking, but my mind keeps going. If I sleep with Apollo that won't take away my visions, won't take away the curse, won't make anyone believe my warnings.

But it might split up Apollo and Nik. For good.

I wish I was sure that would be enough. Even if I break them up, they could be in the same place for another reason. Apollo could still shoot my brother.

"I haven't told you the worst part yet." I have to get away from the idea of sleeping with Apollo. That means moving to idea of my brother being shot by Apollo's arrow.

"It gets worse? Girl, you've been busy over the last few weeks."

"I know. Fate has not been kind. A bit of a bitch, actually."

Julie snorts.

I don't pause to appreciate the humor. "I had another vision. This morning. Right here." I look out at the ocean. My sacred space betrayed me. It allowed the vision to assault me here, allowed Apollo to invade. "I saw Nik shot by an arrow. One of Apollo's weird gold ones."

Julie's face crumples into a wad of confusion.

"Oh. You weren't there. At regionals, Apollo used these crazy gold arrows with white fletching. Just like the arrow that hit Nik in my vision. I watched him die, Julie. Because of Apollo."

Julie is silent. I watch her. Wait.

"Well, that's not going to happen, Kass. It's just ridiculous. Apollo is way too into Nik to shoot him. He's also trying to woo you, or something. Which is creepy, yes. Going after twins? Gross. But he's not going to kill one of you."

I sigh. This curse is dense. Impenetrable. There is no way to push through it, show anyone the disaster looming on the horizon. Julie believed every word of my story. Right up until the part that mattered. I rub the space between my eyes. The pulse of a headache is starting to beat.

Talking isn't accomplishing anything. The only people left I could try to convince with words are Mom and Dad. They won't believe me, either. To them, Apollo is charming, kind, sweet. They will never believe he would hurt Nik, accidentally or otherwise. It's a waste of time and words to try.

"Kass. Are you okay?"

No, I'm not. Nothing is. "I'm exhausted. I feel a headache coming on. I'm going to head home, lie down." I stand and brush the sand from my legs and shorts. "I'll see you tomorrow, okay?"

Julie stands and wraps her arms around me in a huge hug. "Nik's fine. Stop worrying."

I can't. Nik is fine. For now. I just have to find a way to keep him fine. By myself.

Chapter Nineteen

I am empty. I am faded. I drift home, a husk of a girl.

Nik has retreated to his bedroom, probably tucked himself into a ball of blankets and music. I'm glad I don't have to see his face. I don't want to see the anger splashed there.

Upstairs, my room is dark. The curtains I never opened this morning block out what lingers of the sun's light. I close the door and create a quiet, calm, dark, Apollo-free void. I collapse on my bed.

The sleepless night, the vision, the confrontations with Apollo, and the ineffective conversations with Nik and Julie pile on me. They push me down into the mattress, block out my connection to the world around me.

A knock on the door shatters my cocoon, pulls me back to the world. Mom enters my room and settles on edge of my bed. Concern carves her face.

"You okay, kiddo? You've had a lot of afternoon naps lately."

I grip Mom's hand where it rests on my arm. I need that connection to humans, to reality.

"Yeah. I've just been busy. And a little stressed, I guess. Competition. Homework. You know." I rattle off a list of normal teenage concerns for her.

Mom pushes back the curls that struggled free from my hair tie while I slept. "Are you sleeping at night?"

I lie. I nod.

"Okay." A heavy pause while Mom searches my face. "You would tell me if something was wrong. If you needed help. Right?"

I want to tell her everything. I wish she could fix it all for me. That's what moms are supposed to do. Fix everything. But this is so far beyond what any mom can deal with. I can't burden her with it. I can't make her worry about my mental state. So, I do what I've been doing best lately. I smile and nod.

I trail down the stairs behind Mom, determined to slap on a face that passes for happiness and be part of a normal family for one evening.

I pull glasses from the cabinet, plates from the dishwasher. Normal. Normal. Normal.

"Shit!"

I spin to face the island. Mom has a white dishtowel wrapped around her hand. White except for the bloom of red where her fingertip must be swaddled inside.

I forgot.

My eyes shift to the cutting board behind her. Coins of carrot are scattered across the surface. Drops of Mom's bright red blood are splattered across them and the knife she abandoned.

This is my fault.

"Oh, my god, Mom. Are you okay?"

"I cut myself."

I don't tell her that is obvious.

"How bad?" I ask instead.

Mom relaxes her death grip on her finger and unwinds the towel. Please let her finger still be attached.

She prods the injured digit with the healthy fingers of her other hand. Fresh blood pushes to the surface.

"I've had worse. I don't think it needs stitches. The bite I got at work last week was probably worse. Grab me a bandaid?"

I flee the scene of my crime. Again, someone is hurt because I failed to stop it. This time I forgot there was anything to stop. I forgot to protect my mom.

I'm not sure which is worse, knowing that I can't change the fates I see, or being surprised by events I forgot were coming.

They both suck.

There is zero chance I will forget to save Nik. I couldn't forget someone dying in front of me. The question is, can I save him? Can I change his fate?

I return with a box of Band-Aids. Mom is bandaged, carrots are thrown away, dinner is served.

The meal is quiet. Painfully. Nik is absolutely silent, not even a grunt to ask people to pass food to him. He eats what he can reach, gets up, clears his plate, and leaves the room. Without a single word.

I attempt food magic. I push it around in circles on my plate, wanting to make it look like some of it has disappeared.

"All right. What's up with you two?" Dad asks after Nik's silence leaves the room.

"We had an argument. Nik is mad at me. He'll get over it. I hope." This is not the first fight we've had. No one is foolish enough to think it will be the last.

"So why aren't you eating?" Dad points at my still full plate. My attempt at magic has failed.

"I have a headache. I'm just not very hungry." The smile I force feels wan. "I'm going to head up to bed, if that's okay. I'm sure I'll be hungry for a huge breakfast in the morning." I turn the pale smile to Mom. I hope the words do a better job of easing their minds than my face does. Then I realize I just committed myself to being normal at the breakfast table and eating a full meal. Even if angry Nik is seated beside me.

Mom shoos me away from the table with a wave of her injured hand. I know she doesn't mean it this way, but it feels like she is taunting me with my failure.

I pass Nik's room on the way to my own. His door is closed, and I can hear his cello singing behind it. The music tonight is not what he played this afternoon. Tonight's song is softer. Sadder. I stop and rest my hand on the doorknob, tempted to turn it and walk in. I want to fix everything. But to fix everything I have to save him first. Apologies can come later.

I continue down the hall and into my room. I stand in the middle. Lost again. I don't know what to do next. Homework is out of the question. Angles and arguments can't compete with the arrow soaring through my mind every few minutes. I look around my room, searching for inspiration.

My gaze stops on the overloaded bookcase next to my desk. It is crammed with old textbooks, some novels, jumbles of papers, and a massive stuffed gorilla Julie gave me for my fifteenth birthday. I move to the bookcase, scan the titles. It takes only a moment to find the book I am after. MYTHOLOGY blazes down the black spine in gold foil.

I settle into my big comfy chair with the book sprawled open on my legs. I flip through pages, not sure what I am looking for. Anything, I suppose.

I stop at a picture of the marble sculpture of Apollo in Italy. I trail my fingers over the image. It lacks Apollo's silk. I note what the sculptor got right, what he missed. Long and lean, yes. But in reality, Apollo has far muscle than the sculptor gave him. The curls are there, though my Apollo's curls are longer, messier. The face is not even close. My Apollo looks more like a work of art than this marble god. My Apollo's features are sharper, more defined. I force myself to turn the page, move on.

Artemis looks up at me from the next page. I forgot Apollo was a twin. Just like Nik, he has an older twin sister. Artemis, the huntress. I skim the page, remind myself of her story. Artemis saved her brother before he even really existed. When Apollo was trapped inside his laboring mother, Artemis found a safe haven and helped her mother deliver the god. So he could torture me.

I lean back, the book still resting on my lap, and consider my options. Talking to the people involved in the vision accomplished nothing. What if I try other gods or goddesses? Artemis should be invested in her brother's well-being, his happiness. But she has nothing to do with my vision. Maybe she will believe me, believe the risk. Maybe I can convince her to help.

All I have to do is find Artemis. That won't be difficult at all. Just find a goddess and make her listen to what a mere mortal has to say. No problem at all. I sigh.

How can I even find her? Getting pissed and cursing at Apollo had worked to bring him to me. But I have no personal connection to Artemis. I doubt I can call her from the sky.

I look back to the book. Mr. Spanos. Our school's mythology teacher. He is obsessed with myths, with all things Greek. If anyone can tell me how to summon a goddess, it will be him.

I tuck the book away, then take a shower and tuck myself into bed. A sense of something close to peace creeps over me. I have a nugget of a plan. That is better than nothing.

***

I wake in the morning, feeling something close to normal. I am eager to get on with my plan, such as it is. I bound down the stairs and skid to a halt in the entrance to the kitchen.

Nik is already at the island, working his way through a stack of waffles. Shit. I still have to deal with Nik. I have to face his anger, his sense of betrayal.

I sit beside him and pull a waffle onto my own plate. "Good morning." I direct the words to my waffle.

"Good morning," bounces back from Nik. I peek over. He doesn't look at me.

I'll still call it progress. He has shifted from angry avoidance to overly polite, frosty cold. At least he is speaking to me. Well, at me.

We eat in silence.

Hermione leaps onto the island when we are almost finished and settles into a loaf in front of Nik. He holds out his fork, syrup dripping from the tines. Hermione sniffs, then licks the fork. Nik smiles. I smile at his smile. True, his smile is not for me. But he smiled in my presence. We will be okay. Eventually.

***

Mr. Spanos isn't in his classroom before the first bell. My schedule is jammed full, no free hour for me, so I am forced to wait until the end of the day.

Unlike yesterday, which I faked my way through, silent and scared inside my shell, today I am antsy. I can't keep my leg still. Every time I look down, it is bouncing on the floor, on the chair in front of me, on the wall I have propped it against. More than once, someone is annoyed enough to ask me to stop.

So, I start nibbling my lip, peeling the skin from the inside. No one tells me to stop. I make myself bleed before I get that under control.

Today I am present, mentally here. But twitchy.

It would be so much easier if I could see the timer on the bomb I need to diffuse. If I knew how long I have before the arrow sets sail. Since I don't know, I have to act as if it is coming any second. It could be headed for Nik right now.

I ponder burning all the white T-shirts he owns. If I block the only piece of clothing present in my vision will that stop the whole thing?

Only if I burn down every store in town.

And the internet.

The last hour of the day is the worst. English. Mrs. Jacobs is talking about a book. Yet again, I am oblivious to which one. My mind is already in Mr. Spanos' room. I am so anxious to dig into his brain to extract any information that will help me.

The second the final bell rings, I am out of my chair and in the hall. I dodge through the crowd to room forty-two. The last class of the day is still trickling out the door when I get there. Several students linger inside, talking to Mr. Spanos about mythology tidbits I don't have time for. I lurk inside the doorway, waiting for them all to leave, waiting for Mr. Spanos' undivided attention.

Ten long minutes of waiting. Mr. Spanos finally looks at me. Confusion wrinkles his brow. "Kass. You're not in my class this year. Are you?"

"No," I reply. "I just have a mythology question I bet you can answer."

His face lights up. "I'm sure I can help you."

"It's kind of a weird question."

"Hit me."

"If a mortal wanted to talk to a god or goddess, how would they get their attention? I mean, how could they get them to come to earth?"

Mr. Spanos perches on the edge of the desk closest to where I stand. He passes his hand over his head, smoothing hair that isn't there. "That is kind of an odd question. Why do you ask it?"

It hadn't occurred to me he would want to know why I wanted the information. I thought he would just spill whatever I wanted. Of course he is curious, wants to make this into a conversation. I can't tell him the truth, though. I fumble for an answer. "Uhm.... I'm writing a story. For English."

"Ahh. Well. It depends on which specific god or goddess your character wants to speak to. Each of them requires their own individualized invocation, their own unique tribute. The immortal are finicky, you know."

God, do I know. Firsthand. "What about Artemis?"

"Oooo. I hope your character is female. Artemis can only be invoked by a single female or a small group of females. She will not be called or ordered about by any man. She's likely to curse any that try."

I smile. "Yeah. It's a girl. She wants to talk to Artemis alone."

"It's possible, then. It is most likely to work if the girl is a virgin. Artemis is a staunch protector of virginity, both in herself and others."

My cheeks begin to burn. I turn my eyes to the window. This is true of me. Despite Apollo's efforts.

"Ahem," Mr. Spanos continues. "Uhm. She'll need to find a circle of trees with a clear area in the middle. Definitely after dark. Preferably under a full moon. That's when Artemis is easiest to reach." I think back to the early morning I saw Apollo on the beach. Two days ago. The moon had been just shy of full. The full moon must have been last night, or maybe tonight.

"Artemis also requires a poem of sorts. There are a couple of different versions." Mr. Spanos moves to his desk and begins rummaging through a drawer. The surface of his desk is covered with books, papers, and several small statues. The inside of the drawer looks the same. Everything about Mr. Spanos is rumpled and disorganized. "Let me see.... Nope. No. That's the long one. Ooo, here it is."

He turns to me with a single sheet of paper clutched in his hand. "This is one of the shorter invocations, but it should work for your character." He holds the paper out to me. I push aside the thought that Mr. Spanos knows more about calling the gods than anyone really should.

"Can I keep this? Or should I make a copy?"

"You can have it, dear. I'd love to see the story when you are finished, though."

My eyes widen. The only story I've got is the real one. There's no way I'm sharing it with him.

"If you're willing for an old man like me to read it, of course." Mr. Spanos backpedals at the look of terror on my face. I hope he mistakes my horror for embarrassment.

"I'll see how it turns out, okay? Thank you for this. It's exactly what I need." I move quickly to the door, desperate to escape before more awkward happens.

I don't look at the words on the page until I am safely home, shut away in my room. The passage Mr. Spanos gave me is short, a paragraph of text with a citation from Homer scrawled across the bottom of the page. I skim the words. It seems less like a request for a visit from a goddess and more like brown-nosy praise.

I pull out my phone and check the status of the moon. Full last night. I was right. Tonight isn't quite ideal, but I hope it is close enough for Artemis to hear me. She might be my last chance.

Chapter Twenty

Sunset is slow in coming. The sun taunts me, hanging in the sky, strolling slowly toward the horizon. I want to lasso it, pull it down to earth in a fiery ball. But I am a mere mortal. So, I wait.

I claim to be going for another walk. That is technically true. I am on foot, and I'll have to walk around a bit, look for a circle of trees that will serve my purpose.

I take nothing with me other than the sheet of paper from Mr. Spanos tucked into my back pocket. I am glad I don't need any equipment to call Artemis, not even a fire. Carrying a bunch of weird stuff out of the house with me would have made my parents curious, at the very least. I would have had a lot of explaining to do.

The look from Nik as I leave is bad enough. He is on the front porch, settled into the swing with Apollo at his side. Apparently, Apollo has explained away our kiss, convinced Nik he isn't really interested in me. Nik's face suggests the whole mess is my fault, that I made more out of the kiss than it really was.

I hurt Nik for no reason. Apollo is still at his side.

I need Artemis. I need to fight a god with a goddess.

I resist the urge to yell at Apollo; tell him I'm going to tell on him to his sister. I head north, pass The Springs, aimed for a wooded area that lies island from the beach. It is part of The Springs natural area, but is far less beachy, and dry. There are enough trees there, I hope to find a circle of them with space in the middle for me to stand and call Artemis.

Just as the moon slips over the horizon and takes over the sky, I find the spot. An odd clearing, encircled by a ring of trees and ferns. This will work. I sit in the middle and wait for the moon to climb higher into the sky, for its light to fall into my sacred circle.

Once the moon is up and bright enough for me to read without a flashlight, I stand. I call the image of Artemis to mind, imagine her standing before me, her arm pulling the string of her bow back, ready to fire.

I slip my hand into my pocket and pull out the paper Mr. Spanos gave me. I read the words aloud, will Artemis to appear.

"Let me sing of the maiden of contradictions, goddess of the wild chase and the busy spindle. An archer, a hunter, she races through the mountain shadows and the windy hills, drawing her bow and loosing her arrows of sadness. The mountains tremble, and the forest resounds with the agony of animals. Earth and sea both shudder as the strong-hearted one delights in her hunt. And then, when she has had enough, she leaves the forest. Hanging up her bow and quiver, she robes herself in splendor and goes forth to lead her maidens in dance, smiling as they sing of her mother Leto, of how she bore such a wonderful daughter."

I look up from the page. I expect to see Artemis in the circle with me. I am alone. I sigh and turn, wonder what I did wrong, what I missed.

A shooting star burning across the night sky draws my eyes up. The bright light of the moon obscures the stars closest to it, but there is no way to overlook the one in motion. It is large, brighter than the rest, a ball of fire. I watch until it disappears.

"Yes, maiden?"

I spin to the voice on my right. A woman stands at the edge of my circle. The sea breeze toys with the long-layered dress she wears, tossing the fabric gently around her. Long, straight blond hair falls past her waist, sways with the breeze as well, held back from her face by a band of woven leaves. I notice a quiver strapped over her right shoulder, a silver bow clasped in her right hand. They seem insignificant. The beauty overwhelms the warrior.

"Artemis?"

She smiles, gives a single nod. "You called me?"

I lick my lips, unsure how to start now that Artemis is here. I haven't thought this through. I didn't really think I'd get her attention. I doubt leading with 'Your brother is a jerk' will work out well.

"I did." I stall, scramble for a starting point.

Artemis stares at me, one eyebrow raised. "Well?"

"I hope you can help me. I've been having some trouble." I trip over the words. "With your brother."

"Apollo?"

"Well. I guess my trouble isn't with him, specifically. He just caused the trouble. Now I'm trying to figure out how to fix it. Apollo can't, or won't, help. I'm out of ideas. Other than calling you..." I am babbling. I trail to a stop. Take a deep breath.

"How about I start at the beginning. Ish."

Artemis nods. She looks amused. "That might be best."

"I'm a twin. Like you. Apollo visited my brother and I when we were little. He gave me the gift of foresight. His snake also took my arm." I hold up my stump for Artemis to see, as if she had missed it.

"And you want your arm back?" Artemis asks.

"No. That's not the problem. That visit was fine. Well, mostly. The problems started when he came back a few weeks ago. He wants compensation for his gift. He wants my virginity." I pause and watch Artemis' face flicker with an emotion I can't quite identify. Rage? Disgust?

"I told him no." I feel the need to clarify that I didn't give in. "So, he cursed me. Now no one believes my warnings about what I see."

"Apollo." Artemis rolls her eyes. "I'm assuming it gets worse from here?"

She is taking this rather well. As if this happens all the time with Apollo. How many times has Artemis been called on to clean up Apollo's messes? How many other virgins has he toyed with?

"I had another vision a couple of days ago. I saw my brother shot by an arrow from Apollo's bow. Nik died in my vision. I need to stop it from happening in the future. Whenever that might be."

"Well. Don't worry. It won't happen. I've heard my brother mention this boy. He loves him. He wouldn't hurt him."

"Why does everyone keep saying that?" My voice teeters on a yell. "People hurt the ones they love all the time! Love isn't some magic barrier that prevents injury. Most of the time it draws it closer."

Artemis's face turns to a stony glare. I stop my rant. Getting on the bad side of the huntress is not a smart idea.

"I hoped you would believe me. I hoped the curse didn't affect the gods." I don't even try to stop the tears that well. One slips down my cheek.

"I know, he's your brother. You are worried for him. While I don't think the risk is what you imagine, your worry clearly is real. I believe that you believe. And what you believe is your reality. So, to you, your brother is in danger." Artemis chuckles. "I've spent my whole life looking out for my brother, even before he was born."

Her words don't help me at all. She believes me, just not about the part that matters. My heart feels the words, though. They slide over my ache like a balm. "How do I fix this?" I ask. "How do I save my brother?"

Artemis sighs. "I have no idea."

I tug my fingers through my hair, dislodge my ponytail. If even the gods can't help me, there is no chance I can save Nik. No chance I can change his fate. His blood will stain my hand.

"I don't know how to fix this," Artemis continues. "Or if there is even anything to fix. I do know my brother, once again, has meddled with the lives of mortals. I apologize for that. And it warrants a conversation with our father."

"Your father? You mean Zeus?"

"Yes, Zeus. He is our father. He is also incredibly wise. At the very least he should know what Apollo has been up to this time. Perhaps he can help you in some way, ease your fears."

"Can you get him to come here?"

Artemis throws her head back, a rich, hearty laugh spills into the night sky. "No. He will not come to earth for you. But I can take you to see him."

I feel my mouth drop open. I try to cover it by licking my lips. "Uhm. I'm not sure about that."

"Why?"

"He's in Olympus, right?" If the gods are real, and not part of my delusional imagination, Olympus must exist, too.

"Yes."

"In Greece?"

"Yes."

There are so many problems with the idea of traveling to Greece that I don't even know where to start.

"I don't have a passport?" tumbles out my mouth.

Artemis laughs again. "I will take you. You don't need a passport. I can have you back here in less than an hour."

"Really? How?"

"I'm a goddess."

I feel the blush creep up again. Nothing about the gods should surprise me at this point. But I keep underestimating them.

"We'll take my chariot."

"Wait. Was that the shooting star I saw?"

"Yes." Artemis' face pulls me in; I am now her conspirator. "Would you like to take a ride?"

I'm not sure if I'm excited or terrified. A ride in the chariot of a goddess. To Olympus. These words don't even feel real in my brain. My mouth is too dry to speak, so I give a small nod.

Artemis turns, gestures for me to follow. She leads me through the trees to a chariot drawn by two large deer. The chariot is smaller than I expected, just big enough to hold two people standing side by side. Like the goddess's bow, it is made of polished silver. The deer make up for the smaller than expected chariot. They are enormous, larger than I have ever seen. Both have full, large racks of antlers growing from their heads.

Artemis steps up onto the chariot. I follow. On the small platform, my hands grip the edge of the front wall. Nothing about this chariot seems safe. It is enclosed on only three sides, the back left open. I imagine tumbling backwards as the chariot soars across the sky, dropping to my death.

"Home, gentlemen," Artemis says. The deer leap, pulling the chariot with them, up into the sky. I pinch my eyes tightly shut as we speed into motion. I feel like my body was left behind on the ground, only my head and hands still in the chariot. I am afraid to open my eyes, afraid to see the trees and stars speeding past.

The motion of the chariot is so smooth, so gentle, that I am lulled into prying my eyes open. I gasp. We are moving so fast that the land is a blur beneath us. But it's not land at all. It's the sea. The ocean. We are crossing the Atlantic. I pull my mind and eyes away from that thought, look up to the stars. Despite how quickly we move, the stars are still so far away they appear stationary, fixed in the night sky. It is beautiful.

Chapter Twenty-One

———————————————

The sky is falling, taking me with it.

I fight this thought away. The chariot is slowing, dropping altitude. We are okay. Artemis and her deer are in control.

The world below begins to come back into focus. A huge mountain stands in front of us, dotted with patches of snow and trees. I look at Artemis.

"This is Olympus?" I am underwhelmed. I expected something grand. A mansion, maybe. This is a barren mountain.

"Home," Artemis says.

The deer steer the chariot around a tree, and everything changes. Now things are grand. The deer head into a massive stable lit by a multitude of flickering lanterns. Everything inside is gleaming brass or softly glowing wood. Artemis steps down from the chariot and gives each of the deer a quick pat on the flank before she moves toward the door. Who will take care of the chariot? Feed the deer? Isn't that the job of one of the gods? Or am I thinking of a hero? I wish I remembered more from mythology. I drop my thoughts and hurry after Artemis. She moves fast, not looking back to see if I am with her.

We cross a sprawling lawn in front of the largest house I have ever seen. It is so massive that I'm not sure I can even call it a house. The building is nestled into the side of the mountain, overlooking the stable and what seems to be half of Greece.

"Is this your house?" I call ahead to Artemis.

She stops and turns. "This is my father's house. Open to any god or goddess at any time. Each of us has a room, our own personal space here."

It is big, but not large enough to house the multitude of gods that swarm through my brain. "All of the gods live here?"

"No. Not all at the same time. We come and go. The house simply shifts a bit to accommodate anyone it senses on the property."

"Wow." If the house senses me, I wonder how it is shifting to accommodate me.

Artemis turns again, continuing to the house. I can't get my feet to follow. I am stuck, rooted in the yard. I stare up at the mansion in front of me, expecting parts of the building to move. Nothing does.

Artemis crosses the yard then sweep up the marble steps and in through the massive front door as it swings open to grant her admittance. There's the movement I was watching for.

The goddess turns when she is in the door, framed by the light spilling around her. She lifts a hand and gestures for me to follow. Artemis uses a single finger, but I feel it like the pull of a thick cord connected to my navel. I begin to walk. The house seems to grow in front of me as I approach. Given when Artemis said, this might be a true statement.

What have I done? What was I thinking? I am in Olympus. I am headed for a meeting with Zeus, the most powerful of all the Greek gods. He can zap me like a bug if he chooses, if I annoy him. Why would he possibly help me? This is a bad idea.

My head wants to turn me around, run down the mountain and find a way back home. My heart wants to stay and fight to save Nik by any means necessary. My feet decide for us all. They carry me up the stairs to join Artemis in the doorway.

"Try not to be afraid. It's just my dad. He's really not a bad guy." Artemis tries to soothe me. This time her words fail to make me feel better. To Artemis, Zeus is just dad, but to me he is the god of all gods. I can't stop shaking.

Artemis drops her hand onto my arm. "If you want him to listen, really hear you, you cannot appear to be weak."

I close my eyes and take a deep breath. I picture Nik. His face lit by a smile, his body curved in a caress around his cello, his laugh. The image centers me, calms me. I can do this for Nik. I open my eyes.

"I'm ready."

We walk side by side through a large open foyer clad entirely in white marble. Now I get why they use candles instead of electric lights. The bulbs would be too bright against the pure marble, blinding. The candlelight keeps the room from feeling cold and sterile. As it is, our footsteps echo in the cavernous space. There is no fabric to absorb or muffle the sound.

Artemis points me toward a large door, a solid slab of oak, polished to a glowing, warm shine. When we are a foot away, the door begins to move. It swings away from us, revealing a room I have seen once before. It is the room from my dream. I stop and scan the marble benches. I expect to see Apollo draped across one. He is not here. Of course not, he is sitting on a porch swing in Florida, stealing my brother's life.

The only person in the room is a large man with dark hair flowing to the middle of his back. Muscles bulge on his arms, broken only by gold bands around each bicep. He wears an outfit similar to Apollo's dream clothes; a linen garment wrapped around his waist. He does not turn to look at us. I'm not sure he even knows we're here.

Artemis nudges me, gently pushes me across the threshold. I pull in another breath, cross the entrance with one over-exaggerated step. I am literally stepping into the unknown. I expect to be disintegrated into dust with the step.

I look down to make sure I am still here, still intact. The jeans I was wearing when I left the clearing are gone, replaced by the toga-thing draped across my right shoulder. Gentle folds of white fall to my feet. The dress from my dream. My arms fly up to find my hair. It is woven into coiled braids, threaded with laurel leaves. I freeze. Two hands feel my hair. Not one.

"You're welcome." The man in front of me speaks, still not turning to look at me. "I have fixed your flaws, transformed you into perfection."

I am speechless. This is too close to my dream. Was it a dream? Maybe it really was a vision. I will stay here forever, immortal, at Apollo's side. Abandon my family, my mission to save Nik. What if staying here is the one thing that can save him? If I stay with Apollo, maybe I can control him and guide him away from Nik. Keep them apart.

"I assume that's why you are here," the man continues in my silence.

"I didn't want this," I manage. I hold out my new left arm to the man who still refuses to look at me. "I don't consider it a flaw."

He turns then, swings his legs over the marble bench to face me. His eyes land on me, as if he is taking in his adjustments, assessing his work. "You must admit it is an imperfection. One I can fix for you."

I squirm. Being stared at by Apollo had been awkward, as if I were laid bare for him to peruse. Being stared at by Zeus feels different. He is prying into me, looking for my weaknesses, the best point to attack. It is a fight to stand in front of him. I want to turn and run, hide behind Artemis.

Zeus tips his head. "Why are you here?"

I think of my brother. "Nik. I am here for Nik."

"Nik. Your brother."

"I'm trying to save him."

"I don't understand why you came to me. You have Apollo at your disposal." Zeus shifts his gaze to Artemis. "You managed to call Artemis. The two should be more than sufficient to meet any of your needs." His voice turns on the last word, as if anything I might think I need is trivial and far beneath him.

"Your son is going to kill my brother," I blurt. I immediately scrunch my eyes closed, will the words back into my mouth. They don't return, instead they hang in the air above me. I wait for Zeus to drop me on the spot, fry me with a bolt of lightning.

"Really. That seems far-fetched."

My eyes fly open. I am still alive. Zeus is amused by me. His eyes crinkle at the corners, a smile curves his lips. I haven't even told him the whole story, haven't mentioned any sort of vision, and already he doubts me. Already he is blowing me off.

"I am surprised that you, the most powerful of all the gods, are affected by Apollo's curse." These are dangerous words. But I can't hold them back. "I hoped you would be immune."

"I know about the curse, Kassandra. I agree it was... not thought through. But it does not affect me."

Ego. It annoys me.

"You don't believe me. You don't believe Apollo will send an arrow into Nik's chest. Clearly it does affect you." I step forward until I am just a few feet away from the massive man.

"I know my son. He does not tend to wander the world, shooting mortals here and there. Especially mortals he has feelings for." Zeus smiles, then laughs. "He is more likely to pursue them until they run out of energy to resist. Until he wins."

"Nik isn't resisting. I don't know how, or why, I can't see that part. But Apollo will shoot Nik. I don't doubt my vision. Neither should you."

Zeus surveys me again. His eyes brush my skin, pry into my thoughts. I feel him rummaging around in my soul.

"You do seem sincere. You could be crazy, I suppose. Believe your own delusions."

I stand in silence. I can't do anything other than let him judge. I know there are no words to convince him.

"You could take Apollo's offer," Zeus says. "Drink the nectar. Stay here with him."

"I can't." The words are out without a flicker of hesitation.

Zeus stares again. This time his face, his gaze, question me. He doesn't understand why anyone would turn down such a gift.

"Why?" he finally asks.

"I came here to save my brother. Taking immortality for myself doesn't do that. Nik may still die, even if I stay here forever with Apollo. And you. Even if I keep Apollo occupied." Shivers run over me at the thought of what I would have to do to keep Apollo too busy to be bothered with my brother. Delight and despair. "I wouldn't even know if Nik was alive or not. I would be here. Instead of with Nik and my family."

"You can watch them from here." Zeus waves his hand, and a large screen drops from the ceiling. There are no cables, cords, or supports. It floats.

"What is that?"

Zeus snaps his fingers. My house pops onto the screen. The view tightens, zooms in on the front porch and the large window that looks into the living room. Apollo and Nik are no longer on the porch swing. Nik is in his spot, seated on the ottoman, his cello nestled between his legs. Apollo sits in the armchair behind him, his own legs bracketing Nik's hips. Past Nik, Joel and Julie sit side by side on the couch, their hands entwined.

My heart hurts. I want nothing more than to be in that room with them. I want to be snuggled into an armchair. Hear their voices, their laughter. I swallow back tears and shake my head again. "It's not the same. Watching life happen is not the same as living it."

I lock eyes with Zeus. "I belong there. Not here. Having forever to watch them would be slow torture, not a gift."

"Apollo intended this as a surprise for you. He wanted to make you happy here," Artemis offers. I can tell she is trying to make peace, trying to convince me to accept her brother and their world.

I can't. None of this is right. "I'm sorry he doesn't understand. I'm sorry he hasn't loved someone enough to want to do more than watch them."

Artemis moves to Zeus' side and sits next to him on the bench. She leans close to whisper in his ear.

I want to run over, lean in, stick my ear next to Artemis's lips to hear the words that move between them. Instead, I bite my lip and stand still, pretending I am a statue.

Zeus gives one sharp nod. "Hermes!" His voice is barely louder than the volume he used when speaking to me, but it works. A man zips in from a door on the far side of the room. He is as tall as Zeus, but slender. Long, lean muscle cords his body as opposed to the bulk that is Zeus. His movements are quick, sharp. He crosses the large room so fast I would call it a run, though he appears to be casually strolling.

The slender man stops next to Zeus. "What do ya need?"

"The smallest of the black boxes."

Hermes nods. He knows what Zeus wants. I have no idea. Then Hermes is gone, out of the room. He is so fast, so light on his feet, that I don't even hear them strike the stone floor.

I don't know what Zeus has set into motion. A whisper from Artemis. The request for a box. What is in the box? What will it do? How will it change things? *Can* it change things? My fingers twist in the folds of my dress, the only movement I allow while I await the next turn of fate.

"The journey is long. It will only take him a moment." Zeus stares at me as he says these contradictory words. He is looking for something in me.

I don't know what he hopes to find. Maybe he is waiting for me to crack, burst into tears, begging to know what is happening. Waiting for me to beg for my brother's life.

I am about to cave and ask about the box when Hermes returns. He crosses the room again and places a small black box on the bench next to Zeus. It looks like a jeweler's box. I hope it is not a ring that will tie me to Apollo. I want to dart forward, snatch the box, and open it. I grip my dress again to still my fingers.

Zeus lifts the box and rests it on his flattened palm. An offering. "This can help you. But you must use what's inside with intent. You cannot be wishy-washy, or uncertain. You must know what you want and act to take it. Do you understand?"

I have no clue what he means. I want what is in that box. Whatever it is. Zeus is offering me a chance; I just have to figure out how to use it.

Zeus smiles as if my thoughts are written in the air above my head. One eyebrow twitches in amusement. "Good luck, Kassandra." He holds out the box to me.

I step forward, pluck the box with my right hand and pull it tight to my chest. I am desperate to open it, see what is inside. But I resist. A strong reaction of any kind might make Zeus have second thoughts, make him snatch back his gift.

Zeus lets me take the box, then grips my left hand tightly in his own. He holds out the arm, admiring his work. "You really don't want this?"

I look at the arm, then at Zeus. "I've lived without it a long time. I honestly don't know what to do with it." I pause to imagine strolling into my house with two full arms. "And how would I explain it?" I am out of words.

Zeus kisses the back of my left hand. "Too bad. You are exquisite." I'm not sure if he refers to the arm he created out of nothing or to me. Before I can ask, he flutters his fingers along the arm. It disappears.

I stare at the now empty space. I'm not sure if I miss the arm a little or am all glad to have it gone. Artemis taps my shoulder, interrupting my ponder. "It is time to go. I promised to have you back within an hour."

I clutch the small black box in my hand as I scurry to keep up with the rapid pace set by Artemis. I manage one look over my shoulder as we exit the room. Zeus is still seated on the bench but has once again turned his back to the door. His attention is returned to whatever occupied him before I arrived.

The trip back is a blur. Partly because it is hurried. Artemis was serious about her promise of one hour. I am also distracted by the box in my hand. I don't dare open it as the chariot flies through the sky, afraid I will either drop the box or lose its contents.

Artemis lands the chariot back in the woods and steps down. I start to thank her, but glance down to see I am still dressed in the toga. I brush my hand down my torso, careful not to drop the box. "Uhm..."

Before I can say the words, Artemis lifts her bow to the sky. "Dad. You forgot something." I follow the movement of the bow through the air, then look back down. My jeans and shirt are back where they belong. I am toga-free.

"Thank you. I'm not sure how this is all going to end, but I really do appreciate your help." I smile at the goddess.

Artemis gives me a quick hug. "Remember what my father said. Use his gift well." Artemis swallows hard, as if she is holding back tears.

I reach for the retreating goddess. I want to ask her what is wrong, why the thought of me successfully using the gift causes her pain. But Artemis is fast. She is up on her chariot, commanding the deer back into the sky before I can touch her.

Chapter Twenty-Two

Time didn't stop while I was in Olympus. The moon has shifted. The circle of trees is now heavily shadowed. It is too dark for me to clearly see the box I hold in my hand. I was not smart enough to bring a flashlight, so I will have to wait until I am home to open the box, see what I have been given by the gods.

With every step, the box seems to grow heavier in my hand. I try to tuck it in my pocket, make it less substantial in my mind. It doesn't fit. I am forced to carry it, feel the corners, the smooth surface slipping against my fingers, the weight of potential.

From the sidewalk, my house appears to be asleep. The windows are mostly dark, a single dim light burning in the kitchen. I enter the house, expecting to be alone.

As I step into the living room, a lamp flickers on. Mom is curled up on the couch, a cup of tea embraced by her slender fingers. One of them is still wrapped in white.

"Mom." I can't keep the surprise out of my voice. "You're still up." I don't want her to see the box. She will wonder why I returned from a walk with jewelry. Questions will be asked. Where had I been? Who was I with? With nowhere to hide the box, I move into the room and slide into an armchair, tucking the box under my leg as I sit.

"Your dad is snoring. Already. I'm not tired enough yet to ignore it, so I came down for a cup of tea."

I tip my head, direct my ear toward the stairs. I can hear the faint sound of a buzz saw from here. I look back to Mom, a comment about the volume poised on my lips.

"Who did your hair, Kass? It's lovely."

My hand flies to my hair. The braids are still there, coiled around my head in an intricate pattern I would never be able to manage on my own. The good news is the laurel leaves are gone. The bad news is everything else.

"Oh. Uh. Julie. She wanted to practice some options for Delphi Fest."

As soon as the words tumble from me, I know I am in trouble. I had watched Julie from Olympus. She had been here, sitting in the same spot Mom is now in. There is no way she could have done my hair. I am busted.

"I thought you were going for a walk?"

This is not what I expected. Maybe Mom didn't know Julie had been here. Maybe what I saw on the big screen in Olympus had not been real. It doesn't really matter. I don't have a choice; I have to go with the story I have already started.

"I ran into Julie. She walked with me for a bit. Then we sat to talk, and she did my hair." To me, this story makes no sense. Mom knows far less and seems to buy it.

"I haven't seen Julie with you much lately. Is everything okay?"

"She's been spending a lot of time with Joel, I think." I leave out the time I have spent with Apollo, Zeus, Artemis....

"Are you okay with that?" Mom tips her cup to drink the last drops of tea.

I shrug. "They seem happy. I think Nik misses his greatest fan, though."

"He seems to have gained a new one in her place."

"Yeah." I didn't need this reminder of Apollo, how he has wiggled his way into my life.

"You don't like him?" Mom's eyes are sharp. She doesn't miss the frustration on my face.

"I don't dislike him. Not really." I pick my way through the minefield of conversation, afraid I will reveal too much, invite Mom to ask questions I can't answer and can't avoid. "I'm just not sure he's a great match for Nik, that's all."

"It's hard watching your twin find something you haven't found yet." Mom looks out the window. "You had the same difficulty when Nik started playing the cello. Things got better for you when you found archery. I expect the same will happen this time, too." Mom looks back to me, a sweet smile on her face. "You'll find someone to love. Then you'll understand what your brother has, why it works for him."

I wish I could tell Mom how wrong she is. I want to share my real concerns, describe my vision, the curse, all of it. Instead, I play along, take the assumption of jealousy. "Maybe. I guess we'll see. But probably not anytime soon."

"Don't worry, agapitos. You'll find the one who makes your heart sing." Mom stands and crosses the room to me. I feel the box poking into my thigh, trying to wiggle free and jump in front of Mom. I ignore it as Mom kisses me on the forehead and runs her hand over the intricate braids.

"Julie did a great job. It's a shame you have to sleep on it. She'll have to redo it in the morning. Good night, dear. Up to bed soon, and sleep. You need it."

"Night, Mom." I watch her walk into the kitchen. The mug settles onto the counter with a gentle clink before Mom returns to sight and heads up the stairs. She gives me one last wave before she disappears.

I slide my hand under my thigh and pull out the little black box. I turn it in my hand. Better to open this in my room where I am less likely to be interrupted. Or be seen.

I switch off the lamp on my way up. Nik's door is closed, no light peeking underneath. I slip into my own room, close the door tightly behind me, and turn on the lamp next to my bed.

I sit on the edge of the bed, the closed box still in my hand. The urge to quickly pop it open wars with fear over what lurks inside. It could be something that will fix all my problems, give me a way out of the mess Apollo created. It could be something that will make everything worse. Maybe Zeus's solution to the problem is to make me go away. Permanently.

I put the box down on my bedside table and stare at it. Like Schrodinger, I have to open the box to find out what is inside. I reach out to lift the lid. It is tight. Wiggling is required to work it free.

The interior of the box is lined with black velvet. Nestled in the folds is a single small item. I work my fingers under it and lift it from the box. An arrowhead. It doesn't look the smooth steel I am used to seeing in my points. I rub my fingers across the surface. It is stone. Maybe flint. Attached at the base is a metal post with threads running around it. It looks like it will screw into the shaft of an arrow, just like a steel point.

Zeus's words replay in my head. "You must use what's inside with intent. You must know what you want and act to take it."

Zeus wants me to kill someone? With a stone arrowhead? I close my eyes, let the weight of the arrowhead settle into my palm. I didn't understand Zeus's words the first time, and they don't make any more sense now.

He thinks this chunk of stone can help me. Even though I don't get its purpose, I feel obligated to take the god's advice, take his gift, and use it to the best of my ability. I hope that doesn't mean shooting someone.

I tuck the arrowhead back into the box, then stand and move to my closet. I free my archery bag from the depths, and open the zipper, and set my bow to the side. I am after the arrows.

I lift a single arrow from my black quiver, run my fingers along the fletching. I place the arrow between my knees with the point up in the air, grip the cold steel point and spin it until it falls free. In my bag, I rummage until I find my small accessory kit and tuck the steel point inside.

Back on my bed, I sit again, wedge the arrow between my knees. This time the box. My hand stops as it touches the cool surface of the stone arrowhead. Attaching this feels final, an act I can't come back from.

Maybe that was what Zeus meant. Was the act of attaching the head to an arrow a commitment to use it? A display of my intent? Will it be enough to save Nik?

More importantly, what am I committing to do?

I push aside the questions and pull the arrowhead from the box, lift it to the shaft. I close my eyes as I thread the arrowhead, turn it until it locks tightly in place. I'm not sure I can use this arrow the way Zeus intended. But it is ready if I decide I do need it.

I open my eyes and hold the arrow up for inspection. It looks right. Perfect. The gray stone almost looks like the typical steel but has a matte finish that makes the black shaft of the arrow glimmer in comparison. I balance the arrow horizontally on my finger to check the balance. Despite the stone feeling heavy on its own, it doesn't change the overall balance of the arrow.

I need to be able to find this arrow in a hurry, pick it out from the rest in my quiver. In the quiver, I will only be able to see the fletching and a little bit of the shaft. I need to alter this arrow. Mark it. Back to the closet, this time digging for the bulky make-up case I got for Christmas several years ago.

The case is purple and pink plastic, not something I would ever pick out for myself. Not that I ever use it, either. It was a gift from my grandmother. I wipe away a layer of dust, then flip the latch to reveal assorted make-up, nail polish, and jewelry I have accumulated but rarely used. Buried in the bottom of the center compartment is a package of hair chalk.

I pull the green chalk free, moisten the fletching on my Zeus arrow, and stripe it with the green chalk. Again, I hold up the arrow to admire my handiwork. It'll do. The green and white stripes will stand out in the quiver.

I spin the arrow in my hand, watch the green stripes flicker past. Zeus gave me an arrowhead. As a solution to my problems. The primary problem is Apollo's impending shooting of Nik. Did Zeus intend for me to use the arrow on Apollo? He is immortal, a god. Shooting him won't accomplish anything. Will it?

I run my fingers over the stony flint. The edge is sharp. This is a proper, traditional arrowhead, not the rounded points I use for practice and competition. It is definitely deadly. Does it have special powers? Can it kill a god? Stop him in his tracks? Keep him from launching an arrow destined to kill my brother?

I slip the arrow into my quiver and flip the cap closed before tucking everything back into my archery bag and the closet.

I sit on the floor, a puddle of doubt. What did I just do? I feel like I just assembled a bomb. I don't know how long the timer is set to run. When will the explosion come?

Chapter
Twenty-Three

The rising sun carries traditional Greek music on its back. It pummels me awake. Under it, I hear Dad in the hall, clapping and cheering. Without opening my eyes, I can clearly see him dancing his way down the hall.

"Rise and shine, kids! Festival day is here!"

A drum roll sounds on my door, then I hear the same on Nik's next door. I roll over and pull my pillow tight over my head. It does nothing to block Dad's excitement.

The drama of calling Artemis, meeting Zeus, and assembling an arrow of doom has knocked Delphi Fest right out of my head. I forgot today is my day of public display and humiliation.

I sit up, force myself to face it.

Delphi Fest. Dad's favorite day of the year. For him, it's more exciting than Christmas. Delphi Springs always leans toward the Greek, but on festival day, it is over the top. The entire town will be out to celebrate our self-declared status as the most Greek town in the United States. Visitors and tourists will thicken the streets to stew, all eager to see the spectacle.

Downtown will be decorated with olive and laurel branches and swags of white linen. The streets and sidewalks will be crowded with bodies draped in togas of varying levels of authenticity.

Everyone who lives here claims Greek ancestry. My parents can trace theirs, run into ancestors living in Greece within just a few generations. My Uncle Phillip even moved his wife and kids back to Greece several years ago.

For most people in town, this isn't the case. They have to go back dozens of generations, if they can find any Greek ancestors at all. That doesn't stop anyone from claiming to be one hundred percent, pure-blooded Greek. Especially during Delphi Fest. It annoys me. Claiming a culture that isn't your own.

Even worse is the worship of everything Greek, everything that represents the culture. Really it is a worship of the stereotype, not the real thing. That's what the Greek goddess is. The girl who best represents the stereotype of what they think a goddess should look like. I wish I could call Artemis today, let the town see what a goddess truly looks like.

It might be the only way I can get out of this day.

I don't think she would appreciate it.

A vision replaces my mental picture of the actual Greek goddess with the image of a Greek god. Apollo sits on my bed, the covers a tangled mess around him. My pillow is tucked between his back and the wall. My head is nestled on his chest, using him as a pillow. His arm is wrapped around me, tucking me tightly into place.

I blink and it is gone.

What the hell?

Apollo in my bed. With me sleeping by his side. In his arms.

He looked cozy. At home.

So did I.

No.

This vision hurts almost as much as seeing Nik shot by Apollo's arrow. Nik's wound was physical. Mine is emotional.

I wouldn't sleep with the enemy.

Would I?

I've faced that temptation and won. There's no way I would cave now. Not with my brother's life on the line.

Add my heart to the list of things I need to guard. The things I need to protect from Apollo.

I drag my carcass down the stairs. Nik is in the living room. He looks as thrilled about this day as I feel. He stands on an ottoman with both arms outstretched. A scarecrow-mannequin.

Dad is in front of him, draping a bed sheet over Nik's clothes. Dad always insists on togas for Delphi Fest. Nik and I stopped protesting years ago. It is easier to just go along with it, humor Dad.

I smile up at Nik. He rolls his eyes over Dad's head. And just like that, we are at peace. The argument over Apollo and his questionable intentions pushed aside. Apollo is my problem, not Nik's. I'll solve it without dragging Nik through any more agony. And without climbing into bed with him.

I check what Nik is wearing under his toga. Shorts and a blue shirt. No white shirt. He is safe. For today.

Apollo's arrow will have to wait for another day.

***

Downtown is jammed full of toga clad torsos. Bodies press against me as we worm our way through the crowd to Sponge Brothers.

My face looks back at me, hanging in the front windows of the restaurant next to the other nominees. It is very strange to look at myself in the past. I am used to seeing things in the future.

Dad drags us to the voting booths. I duck my head, avoid eye contact with the crowd around us. I don't want to match the face in the window.

Whispers still surround me. "Look, that's her." "What happened to her arm?"

It is all the bad of being a celebrity without the good. No paycheck.

I vote for Julie, then flee. "See you later. I'm going to go get ready," I call to my parents and slip into the crowd.

I wind my way down the sidewalk to Spartan Sweets. Julie is framed in the front window, already draped in her toga, hair coiled on her head. She sits on the counter next to the register with Linda beside her. I can't hear them through the glass, over the crowd, but I can see Julie chattering away. Linda smiles and nods periodically. Everything in there is so normal.

That's what today is. A chance for me to have my version of normal, just for a moment. No more visions, threats, or arrows.

"Sorry I cut it so close," I say once I am in the sugar laden haven. "Chaos at home, as usual." The door swings shut behind me, cutting off the murmur of the mass of people outside.

Julie drops from her perch and wraps me in a hug. "I'm so happy we're nominated together! I know you're gonna win, but I don't care."

I want to argue, tell her she'll win, but Julie doesn't give me a chance, pushes me into a chair by the front window so that the late morning sunlight spills across my face.

"Sit. We need to fix your hair and make-up." Julie reaches for her huge bag on the table. It is nestled in a thicket of curling irons and brushes on the table's surface.

"Linda, are you sure you're okay with us taking over the shop like this?" I ask.

"Yep. You guys in the front window will draw a lot of attention. I'll be crazy busy later with tourists that want to eat the sweets the goddesses eat." Linda smiles at her words. "I should make that part of an advertising campaign."

Julie laughs. "I bet you could get the pics from Sponge Brothers and hang them in here. They usually give them to the nominees, but I'll give you mine."

"You can have mine, too." I add. Last year's picture is somewhere in my room. Probably the back of my closet, facing the wall. I should pull it out for target practice in the backyard. That's about all it's good for.

I look around the shop, trying to imagine my picture hanging here with the other girls. Where are the other girls? "Hey, where is everyone else?"

"At Sponge Brothers," Julie answers. "Kurt said all the contestants could use the restaurant to get ready. We'd already told Linda we'd be here, so, here we are."

"It's weird that we're not all together." I am sure some of the girls will hold this against me, think I am separating myself because I think I am special. Because they think I think I've already won. That I deserve to win.

I sigh and resign myself to the day. I close my eyes and let Julie do her thing. She is obsessed with making other people gorgeous. She always looks great herself but seems to enjoy making others shine even more.

Julie runs a one-sided stream of conversation while she brushes color across my face. It is the best kind of conversation. I don't need to form proper responses. Nods and grunts suffice. I don't hear much of what Julie says. My mind darts to Olympus, to the arrow tucked away in my closet.

"Look," Julie commands. "Good?"

I open my eyes. Julie holds a mirror in front of my face. The Greek goddess from my dream looks back at me. Her hair is less intricate, twined into a low-slung bun with twists of curl framing her face. But the make-up is spot on. I furrow my brow. So does the goddess in the mirror.

"Is it bad?" Julie asks.

"Oh. No." I put my hand on Julie's arm. "It's great. It just reminded me of a weird dream. Thanks. It's great."

A sharp knock on the glass window turns both of our heads. Mom is on the other side, waving. We wave back, which she takes as an invitation to come in.

"Are you two ready? Voting closes in ten minutes. The other girls are already at the stage. You've got less than thirty minutes until crowning." Mom steps closer, examining our hair and make-up.

"Why didn't you do Kass's hair the way you had it last night?" she asks Julie. "It was so beautiful."

Confusion flickers over Julie's face for a split second before she tucks it under a smile.

"I just decided simple would be better. Plus, Kass was kind of late getting here. I was worried about the time." Julie is so sincere with her words, so smooth. Mom doesn't notice the moment of confusion, the fumble to cover.

Once the words are past her lips, Julie turns to me, one brow raised in a look that demands answers later.

I give her a smile. "We should probably get outside, right? They'll send a squad looking for us soon." I stand and move to the door; hold it open to let Julie and Mom exit first. "Thanks, Linda! Get ready for the surge of hungry tourists."

I follow Mom down the sidewalk, back to Sponge Brothers. Now I am grateful for the crowd, the bustle, the hands that steer Julie and me onto the stage beside Mirabelle and the other nominees. Julie can't ask me questions. I know I'll have to explain; I just need time to decide what I want to tell Julie. She believed me about Apollo, but traveling to Olympus in Artemis's deer-drawn chariot might be harder to swallow. I suppose I could lead with the vision of me sleeping in his arms. I'm sure Julie would be totally on board with that one.

On stage, I scan the crowd. I find my parents, Nik, Joel, and a slew of other familiar faces in the swarm of bodies from out of town. I don't see the face I am looking for. Apollo isn't here. My shoulders rise. Apollo's absence combined with Nik's blue shirt means Nik is safe. At least for now.

I pull my focus back to the stage just in time to catch Kurt's announcement of my name. Julie wraps me up in a quick hug, then turns me around and nudges me toward Kurt and the crown he holds. I won.

I step toward Kurt to accept. I would love to decline, but that would bring an even worse brand of attention. Kurt settles the crown onto my head. It is more of a headdress, a woven band of olive and laurel branches. He kisses me on the cheek. I paste a smile on my face and turn to wave to the crowd.

Kurt murmurs to me, his microphone no longer on. "Jesse should be in front of Spartan Sweets with the float. Head on over and get ready to roll." He shifts to look at the other nominees, still on stage. "Who do you want to ride with you as your attendant?"

I turn to look at the girls behind me. Mirabelle points to Julie. They all know who I will choose. I nod. I am surrounded by the girls in a quick group hug, murmurs of congratulations floating around me. They drift away, off stage and back to their lives. Within a minute, only Julie and I remain.

I step down from the stage, Julie right behind me. We make our way through the crowd. This time there is no chance of hiding. I am the goddess.

The float isn't in front of the sweet shop. Julie grabs my arm and pulls me inside the store. We beat the bulk of the crowd; the shop is still empty. Linda is tucked away in the back room. Julie moves so she is between me and the door, blocking me in.

I don't have words ready.

Chapter Twenty-Four

"What gives, Kass?" Julie stands in front of me, her arms crossed over her chest.

"Last night I told my mom you did my hair. It's really not a big deal." Honesty with a touch of underplay. It's the best I've got.

"Okaay," Julie draws the word out. "Who did your hair, then? Why tell your mom it was me?" A pause.

"Where were you that you shouldn't have been?"

She is scary good at finding the heart of the story. I decide to skirt the truth, give Julie some bits of reality. "It was Artemis."

"Artemis?" Julie is completely confused. I can see her mentally flipping through all the girls at our school, trying to find an Artemis.

"Apollo's sister." I pause to let Julie catch up. "She came to talk to me last night."

"And she did your hair." Julie does not look like she believes me, but there is no way I can convince her of the truth, that Zeus is the one who had fashioned a nest of intricate braids for me. Without touching me. While I was in Olympus.

So I nod. "Yeah. I asked her for advice for dealing with her brother."

Julie just stares at me, as if she is waiting for the eruption of maniacal laughter.

"Did she have any?" she finally asks.

"Not really. Not anything helpful." That was the truth. Artemis hadn't given me advice or help. That also came from Zeus.

Julie sighed. I don't think she believes any of it, she has just given up. "Next time try to warn me. I can do a better job of keeping your secrets, whatever they are, if I know what's going on."

Over Julie's shoulder, something that must be the float pulls into view at the curb. Saved by the parade float?

"I think our ride's here," I say. "Our chariot awaits."

We move out of the shop, leaving the unsatisfying conversation behind us.

I reach to adjust my headdress.

"Don't mess up your hair!" Julie swats my hand to save the twisty bun and spiraling curls from my probing fingers.

It itches. I want it off.

Julie grabs my hand and pulls me toward the float waiting at the curb. The "float" is really a rusty red pick-up truck wrapped in cardboard panels and sheets of linen. Olive branches and flowers complete the camouflage. It's far less than the chariot I rode in last night.

A man stands on the sidewalk next to the truck. Ratty jeans. A green hoodie.

Hoodie Guy is our chariot driver. Jesse? Was that the name Kurt used? Today the green hood is dropped down, lying on the man's back. His brown hair is a tangled mess that looks like it hasn't seen a brush this week. I am jealous. He looks comfortable and relaxed. No one will be looking at him, scrutinizing. Judging.

Then he sees me. I see the flicker of recognition dance across his face. He gives me one short nod of his chin to acknowledge that he knows who I am. He remembers what I did.

I saved him. That's what I do. I will save Nik, too. And hopefully myself.

"Up. We're late." Julie pushes me toward the bed of the truck, nudges me to climb up and take my place.

I lift the folds of my toga in my hand and use my stump to brace against the side of the truck as I clamber up. Julie jumps up beside me and rearranges the folds of my toga.

"Perfect. Just like last year," Julie says.

It does feel like deja vu. This is exactly how this went last year. With the bonus of the Apollo mess.

"I don't know why I got nominated for this again. Or why I won. Again. I'm just glad it will be the last time."

"You are the vision of Greek goddess perfection, Kass. Enjoy it!" Julie manages this without a trace of jealousy in her voice. She really is happy for me.

I try to enjoy it for her. I smile and wave to a group of women walking past on the sidewalk. Time to start the show.

"If only she weren't missing an arm." This drifts up to me from the clump of women.

"She would be perfect. Such a shame." It's as if they think I'm missing my ears in addition to part of my arm.

My cheeks flame. I look away, turn my back on the gossipy group. This is what I hate most about this day. All the stares and attention reach maximum intensity. I am on display, as if I asked to be judged. I didn't nominate myself for this.

I wish this float were part of a large parade. I could hide in the swirl of all the other girls' togas, lose myself in the noise of a marching band.

Instead, it is just this sad little truck. Just me and Julie. Nowhere to hide.

My family stands a block away on the sidewalk, all dressed in togas. Dad looks giddy. He bounces from foot to foot and nudges Nik, trying to pass his excitement to his son. Dad peers down the street in my direction. I think he's trying to get a glimpse of me in all my goddess glory.

He doesn't see the excessive drinking and rowdiness that surround him, disguised in the stereotype of Greek celebration. He doesn't see the judgment directed at me. Dad only sees a perfect Greek woman claiming her rightful place of honor.

Jesse the Hoodie Guy thumps the cab of the truck, the only spot other than the front windshield that isn't covered. "Ready? Movin' out!" He slides into the cab of the truck.

"Time for the fun!" Julie says. She looks out into the crowd. I can tell the moment she finds Joel. She beams. I turn to look at Joel. He is looking at Julie like she is his goddess.

The truck lurches into motion, the engine clearing its throat as Jesse changes gears.

I keep my stump on the roof of the cab for balance and lift my hand to wave. A deep breath. A pasted smile. Fifteen minutes. I can do anything for fifteen minutes.

I wave. The crowd of residents and tourists wave back, yell, cheer. There is so much human noise that I can't hear the rolling of the waves on the beach two blocks over. I miss it.

My eyes land on a man in the crowd. All the noise and chatter stop. I am wrapped in total silence, my eyes locked with Apollo's. He is in his muted, almost human skin. His toga-less form stands out in the crowd. Dark jeans, white shirt, dark denim jacket. Gorgeous enough to glow against the crowd around him, not quite gorgeous enough to raise suspicion.

He draws his left hand from behind his back. His bow is clutched in his grip. Is this the moment? The moment he shoots Nik? Nik isn't wearing a white shirt. He is wearing blue under his toga. Could my vision have gotten that detail wrong? Why shoot Nik now? There is no reason, it is too random, even for a fickle god. My mind flies to the arrow tucked in my closet. Useless. I would give anything to have my bow in my hand, the arrow nocked into place.

My hand keeps waving, driven by a motor separate from the rest of me. The remainder is still, every cell watching Apollo as the truck rolls past. He smiles. Winks. I flinch and blink, breaking the spell. Sound pours back into the day.

I turn my head, try to recapture Apollo in my sights. He is gone. I strain, seeking him in the crowd. What is he doing? Who is he threatening with his golden bow? Maybe he knows I went to Olympus and talked to Zeus. Maybe he wants me dead. Did I save Nik and sacrifice myself?

I don't find Apollo again until the truck skitters to a stop, the float ride at an end. We are back in front of Spartan Sweets, the circle of downtown completed. My family is still on the sidewalk where I left them.

I jump from the bed of the truck, ignore Julie's call after me. I run, pushing bodies out of the way, trip over my toga and almost sprawl on my face on the sidewalk in front of Mom.

"Kass!" Mom stops my fall with a hand on my arm. "What's wrong?"

I spin in her grip. I find Dad, Julie, Joel. Then Nik. He stands at the sidewalk's edge; his hand twined in Apollo's. I don't see Apollo's bow, but I know it's here, maybe tucked under his jacket. I feel it hanging over me. Over Nik.

"Kass." Mom pulls me back around, forces me to meet her eyes. "What is the matter with you?"

I look back over my shoulder. Nik is still okay. "I just thought I saw..." I trail off. Could I have imagined the whole thing? Maybe I only thought I saw Apollo, his bow, the wink.

"What, honey?" Mom smooths the hair back from my face that tumbled loose in my sidewalk scurry.

"I don't know." I hate this. I hate the threat of fate. It is taking over my brain, driving me crazy.

"Nothing, I guess." I take a deep breath, try to calm my breathing. I need my bow. Without it, I don't have any options. I can only watch Nik. Watch Apollo. I can only watch and hope I will be armed and ready when it is time to change fate.

I turn from Mom to look at Nik again. There is no way to stop my eyes from seeking him. He is oblivious to my flight up the street, my near crash. He is wrapped up in conversation with Apollo. Apollo doesn't look my way, either, but I know he knows exactly what happened, heard every word of my conversation with Mom. I glare at his profile, will him to turn and take it. He doesn't. A wasted glare.

Julie steps to my side, pulling Joel along with her. "You okay?"

I nod. "Are you guys ready to go?" I ask the group, my voice loud enough to force Nik and Apollo to hear me, acknowledge me.

"I'm hungry," Nik says. "I need dolmades. And baklava."

"I'll buy," Apollo offers. He includes me, my parents, Julie and Joel in his hand-wave gesture.

"We'll split it," Dad counteroffers.

The deal is done. We begin the trek down the still crowded sidewalk. Apollo leads us, heading for the food truck parked just down the street from Sponge Brothers and the temporary stage that is slowly disappearing. There is no way to get out of this meal, no way to drag

Nik home to the safety of my bow and Zeus's arrow. I trail at the back of the group, a seventh wheel at the tail of a caravan of couples.

Another meal with Apollo as a guest of my family. I am tired of watching these. This time my silence is unnoticed. The trio of couples are deep in conversation within their pairings. Each pair remains solitary, not interacting with the other couples.

I am the odd. No one notices me sitting quietly, picking at my dolmades, unwrapping the grape leaves and shredding them into confetti in my basket.

By the time the herd is ready to move, most of the day has drifted away. Sunlight slants across the table, dusk heavy on its heels. Mom finally sees me. I must have a look on my face. I try to cover the mixture of fear and hatred I feel mingling on my features, but I am not fast enough. Mom's face erupts into sympathy. I feel it stretch down the table to rub my shoulder.

Mom probably thinks I am jealous of Nik's relationship with Apollo, maybe even jealous of Julie and Joel. I twist my lips into a smile. Even I don't buy it. It's better for Mom to think I am jealous than for her to know the truth. Right now, I am imagining the gratification of seeing Apollo dead at my feet.

The parade of couples starts again, this time heading for the Pitera house. Julie and Joel peel off after a couple of blocks, headed to Julie's. Without them, I am more obviously out of place. Mom tries to include me in conversation, but Nik and Apollo are in their own universe. They have clearly marked the boundaries of their coupledom and are not taking visitors.

Apollo walks all the way to our house. I wish he would vanish. Instead, he settles on the porch with Nik while the rest of us head inside. I don't want to leave them alone. I want to wiggle onto the swing between them, keep them from touching each other.

That would be inappropriate. So, I head up to my room, leave the lights off, and pull my bow and arrows from the closet. I strap on my release and slide my window open to sit on the windowsill. Armed eavesdropping is appropriate. In this case.

I can't lean far enough to see them on the porch below me, but I can hear the soft murmur of their voices. Only a few minutes pass before I hear the creak of the swing, then see Apollo step into view down onto the front sidewalk, turn and wave goodbye to the invisible Nik on the porch. Apollo moves toward the street, then turns and looks over his shoulder, his eyes shooting directly to me. I freeze; hope I blend into the shadows of the rapidly darkening day. He sees me. I feel his eyes travel over my skin, burn a trail down my arm. He smiles, then turns and walks away.

I sit in the window until his figure blends into dusk. I stay another hour, waiting for him to return, threaten my family. Fatigue steals me. I jerk, almost tumbling out of the window, on the edge of literally falling asleep. I am done. Apollo is gone, hopefully finished lurking for the day. I climb into bed, still dressed.

Alone.

Chapter Twenty-Five

F ingers smooth over my face, run through the loose tendrils of hair spun across my cheek and pillow. I smile into the slide of silk over my skin. I take a deep breath and smell the storm-tossed sea.

Apollo.

My eyes snap open and I push away, press my back against my headboard and pull my knees up to my chest. These are frail protections. I hold in the scream that threatens to burst free, let out only the gasp pushed out by my heart scrabbling up my throat.

He sits on the edge of my bed. Calm. He holds up his hands palm out to me to show me he is innocent. Harmless.

I know better.

I dive around him to the floor, throwing the covers that dangle from the edge of my bed next to Apollo. The bow I left beside my bed. I need it.

"Looking for this?" Apollo flicks on my lamp and nudges the object peeking out from under the bed near my bedside table.

I sit back on my heels near the foot of the bed. I look longingly at the bow by his feet. He is between me and my weapon. The strap that still dangles on my stump is useless without it.

Apollo lifts his feet from the floor and scoots back on my bed, giving me a clear path to my bow. "Go ahead. If it will make you feel better, I want you to have it."

I watch him, wait for him to jump off the bed and attack. It is the path to the mineral pool. This time lined with Apollo instead of snakes.

Apollo tucks his feet under him, pulls my pillow over and fluffs it before tucking it behind his back. He is making himself at home. On my bed.

This is where he was in my vision. Nestled onto my bed. In my space.

I will not join him.

I crawl across the floor, but keep my head up, my eyes on Apollo, as I move to my bow and pull it free.

"You know, you shouldn't sleep with your window open, anyone could climb in." Apollo watches me as I lift Zeus's arrow and click it into the nocking loop. "That's new." His face remains calm, unconcerned, a gentle smile on his face.

Either he doesn't know I went to Olympus and got the arrowhead from Zeus, or he doubts I will be able to use it against him. I doubt it myself, but I feel better with the arrow in my hand, loaded into my bow, ready to fire.

"What do you want?" I ask the god on my bed. Again, tonight, he is showing me the full version of himself. Nothing is turned down. At least this time he is fully dressed, still in the clothes he wore to Delphi Fest.

It's a bit of a relief. A half-dressed god in my bed might be too much to bear.

"I don't know." Apollo shrugs. "I just wanted to see you. You were lovely today. But by the end it looked like the day wore you down."

Does he not know he is the source of all my tension? That he is the weight bound tightly to my neck, choking me?

Apollo tips his head. "What?" He looks genuinely confused and concerned by my distress.

"I don't understand you. You are lovey-dovey all day with Nik. At least when you're not standing in a crowd waving your bow at me. You didn't speak to me at all. Just lurked. Threatened. And now here you are. On my bed. Worried about me? It doesn't make sense."

He shrugs at me. I don't know which I hate more: the conspiratorial winks or the innocent shrugs.

"I'm complicated. I've had a long time to grow and develop. I've moved past the limits of human emotion, I guess. I am capable of having feelings for more than one entity at a time."

"I prefer to think of myself and my brother as humans. Not entities."

He shrugs again. The shrug is winning.

"If you're so emotionally advanced, why don't you understand I can't share you with my brother? My feelings make that a no go. Ever. Even with a god."

He smiles at me. A new entrant in the contest for my hatred. "I do love you, you know."

I cut my eyes to his. He said before he didn't love me. Now he does? Even though the words don't quite make sense, they still seep in. Soak the rocky compacted soil bunched around my heart.

"It's different than the love I have for Nik." He heard my unasked question. "My love for him is clean. My love for you is tinged... that's not the right word. It has an undercurrent. A thread I can't quite identify."

I can't face these words head on. My gaze drifts away. I understand him. I don't like it. I am drawn to him, like a moth to a flame. Even though I know he will destroy me, destroy the people I love. The attraction is complicated. For both of us. "Ahh. I'm a puzzle to you. Something to figure out."

"That's not what I said." Apollo's voice is sharp, pulling my attention back to him.

"You said this-" I point at Apollo then myself, "is something you can't identify."

"The relationship. Not you. You I understand. What I don't understand is why I am drawn to you."

"Maybe it's genetic."

Apollo narrows his eyes as if he is trying to bring my words into focus. He fails.

"What do you mean?" he asks.

"Nik and I are twins. Maybe there's something in our DNA that is like catnip for you."

"Hmm. Interesting..." He stares, then shakes his head. I have been compared to Nik and found lacking. I think.

"I don't think so," Apollo says. "The draw to you is different than the draw to your brother. I think that rules out a genetic commonality."

"You're talking about this like it is something your brain controls. Love is all heart. You do have one of those, right?" I know he does. I've heard it beat. I want to crawl to his side and press my ear to his chest, listen for the steady thump again. Let it pound into me like the waves of the ocean. My vision lies down that path.

I swear the man is a snake charmer and I am his snake. I still hold my bow, the arrow ready to draw, but my arms are loose, relaxed at my sides. My hand and bow rest calmly in my lap. I am not weaponized.

My mind sees Apollo as a threat. My body, my heart, clearly feel differently.

My heart is winning.

Apollo melts a touch. He can feel my change in mood. "Come here, Kassandra."

I want to blame it on the pull, the pull I felt when Artemis called me, gestured me toward the door at Olympus. With Artemis the pull connected to my navel, drew me toward the goddess. Tonight, the pull is higher. It tugs in my chest.

It is not just the pull. Apollo does not force me. I choose him.

My vision merely showed me sleeping in Apollo's arms. I'm not sure it was really a vision of disaster. Other than puncturing my heart again, twisting the dagger a little more, what is the risk? If I'm twined in Apollo's arms, he can't use them to shoot my brother.

I leave my bow on the floor as I cave and climb onto my bed, tuck into his side. He wraps his arm around me and pulls me close, settles my head on his chest where it belongs. Apollo stretches an arm to pull the comforter over me. He tucks me in.

I breathe him in, the metronome of his heart setting our rhythm. I sink lower into myself, into us, drift to the very edge of sleep.

Apollo runs his fingers over my hair, down my spine, hums me to sleep.

"You won't be able to use it, you know." I hear the whisper as my lids slip shut.

I fall into dreams of the words. I see myself over and over, Zeus's arrow drawn, Apollo in my sights. Every time, I fail to shoot him. The bow falls from my grasp, I shoot the arrow wide, he deflects the projectile, or I stand frozen, unable to release the arrow at all. Over and over through the night I relive my failure to save my brother. The only upside is I never see Apollo fire. Never see his arrow sink into Nik's flesh.

Chapter Twenty-Six

I miss the warmth of Apollo before I even remember I fell asleep wrapped in it. I miss the strength of his arms around me. It is not something I should want, but I can't help it. I do. I roll into a ball and pull the covers up under my chin. They smell of the sea. He lingers.

There is nothing right about my relationship with Apollo. It is based on deception and curses. It involves my brother in a way that is weird. And a little sick.

Apollo was in my room last night. It is hard to wrap my mind around, even with his lingering scent. I shifted from the burning need to kill him on the spot to complacency that let me sleep in his arms. Even though I had a vision warning me that it would happen. That scares me. I have no idea what the repercussions of that choice might be.

He seemed to know about the arrowhead his father gave me. He doubts my ability to use it. Were his words as I drifted off another curse? Or just a subtle suggestion to make me doubt myself. Or a simple statement of the truth.

My dreams were plagued with uncertainty. Failure. Yesterday I was sure I could shoot Apollo if I needed to. Today I'm not sure I can let the arrow fly. I would do anything to protect Nik, but I can't imagine being angry enough to shoot Apollo. Even with an arrow that I don't think can kill him. He is immortal, after all.

It might hurt him.

Which would hurt me. Even fear for Nik, for his life, might not be enough to push me to hurt someone else. Especially when that someone has a crazy, stupid connection to me. To my heart.

I roll over, dodging the thoughts I dislike.

My bow and arrow sit neatly on the bed beside me. Next to my release strap. Apollo must have taken it off my stump, tucked it next to me with my weapon before he left. I trail my fingers over the cold stone arrowhead. Apollo is so sure I won't use it that he feels comfortable taunting me with it.

I may not be sure I can use it, but I intend to keep it close. It will travel with me today, and every day, until I save Nik. I won't risk being caught without it, not after yesterday's panic in the parade.

This is a vision I won't have to hunt down. I was in it, with Nik. I don't have to search for Nik, search out Apollo and his bow. I can do whatever, really. The event will come to me.

I'm mostly sure that's how this will work.

I'm completely sure I'm not convinced I can change what I saw.

I strap the release back onto my stump and tuck the arrow into the quiver. Quiver over shoulder, bow in hand, I head down to the kitchen. I didn't eat much yesterday. I am starving. I need fuel for the unknown battle ahead.

On the island is a note from Mom, scrawled on the back of a flier from the vet's office.

Breakfast date. Then grocery store. Back in a couple of hours. Love you guys, Mom and Dad.

The note pulls a smile to my face. Their dates are cute, if I can pretend all they ever do is eat and talk.

Next to the note from Mom are two ivory envelopes. One has my name scrawled across the front; the other has Nik's. I don't recognize the handwriting. It is twirly, swirly. Beautiful. It looks like calligraphy.

I lift the envelope with my name. It is heavy in my hand, the paper thick. My finger slips under the flap to free the card inside. Plain, no picture on the front, just a rich, heavy card stock filled with writing on the inside. The same rolling, curvy hand that had written my name on the front fills the inside.

My eyes skim over the words to find the signature at the bottom. *All my love, Apollo.* I look around the kitchen. How long did he stay last night? Did he sit here this morning, sip a cup of coffee while he talked to my parents and nibbled on a donut? It wouldn't have mattered if he had no explanation for his presence in the house with both Nik and I asleep upstairs. Mom was so into the image he projected to her that she wouldn't notice anything was wrong. Off.

I focus on the script, force my eyes back to the beginning, read every word.

Dearest Kassandra,

Thank you for last night. For giving in to the connection we share, if only for a moment. It helped me decide what I truly want, what I need.

I need you.

Together we are something amazing. You force me to be my best, in every moment. I need that push.

I know I have asked before. I am asking again. Please consider forever. You know how easy it would be for me to give to you; what you stand to gain. I want to be eternally yours.

I will see you soon.

All my love,

Apollo

My hand falls. The card slips free and skitters across the island. He interpreted last night as a promise that I would give in to what he wanted. He still thinks he has a chance to win me, take me away from my family. My life.

After my choice last night, I am worried he might be right.

I snatch up Nik's card, hold it in my hand for a moment. What does this one say? Is it an offer for Nik to join us as an awkward, gross trio? I ignore the stab of guilt and open Nik's card.

Nikolas,

I love you. You know I do. You own a piece of my heart no one else will ever be able to touch. I would like to think I have claimed a piece of yours in exchange.

But I am more than that one piece of my heart. The larger bits of me need something you cannot provide.

I will remember you for all of eternity.

Love always,

Apollo

I narrow my eyes. A Dear John letter? A god with the experience of ages and that is the best he can do? A vague, it's not you, it's me-ish letter to break up with the person he claimed to love above all others.

There is no way I can let Nik see this note. No way I can let Apollo break his heart like this. If Nik never sees the note, he will think Apollo just disappeared, leaving him in the lurch like a jerk. Nik will think it was just a fling that had run its course. Eventually he will heal. It will be a shallower wound than this note that suggests he doesn't matter enough to Apollo, that he lacks something Apollo needs.

I clutch the two notes in my hand along with my bow and head out the door to the back yard. The day is clear, crisp. The opposite of the muddle in my head. The ocean calls the second I step outside, attempts to soothe me.

I continue to storm.

I cross the back yard to a large target attached to a block of foam. Two notes find themselves pinned to the target, with me facing them from the opposite end of the yard.

I reach back and pull an arrow from my quiver. Solid white fletching. A normal point on the tip. I nock the arrow and attach the release. Draw. Focus on Apollo's Dear John note through the sight.

My jaw shifts, sends the arrow flying across the yard. It lands with a satisfying "thunk" in the center of Apollo's note. A tiny bit of my anger goes with it.

I grab another arrow, again with solid fletching. This arrow also sails true, landing deep in Apollo's love note to me. It is not as satisfying as I wish it to be. I need to feel it burrow in, hurt Apollo.

I pull a third arrow. Stripes. I spin the arrow in my fingers, debate for a moment before nocking and sighting the love note again. The stripes travel straight and true across the yard. The arrowhead slices through the heavy paper of Apollo's note.

That feels better.

I close my eyes, finally let the sound of the waves wash over me, wash away some of the tension and stress.

When my eyes flicker open, Apollo stands in my yard. He is at the edge of the grass, close to the house, and out of the arrow's path. A full-blown god stands before me. Apparently today he doesn't care if mortals see him. If they know what he is.

The only god-thing missing is his toga. He is wearing worn jeans and a black T-shirt with the logo of a heavy metal band. In one hand he holds his bow and a single arrow. In his other hand he holds a water bottle.

"That seems excessive," he says. He nods at the arrow sticking out of the target. Out of his words.

I want that arrow back. Without it, I am armed only with words of my own.

"What do you want?" I say. These are flimsy weapons.

"I thought my note made that clear." Apollo looks at the target again, takes a few steps toward it. "You read the note I left for Nik? That wasn't intended for you."

"After I read your note to me, I needed to know what you said to him. I need to know how to protect him. From you."

I take a step to the side, trying to find an angle to get me to that arrow. Apollo mirrors my movement.

"I didn't think you would dare to show up here. Nik's right inside, you know." I can't imagine Apollo would want to see Nik right now. So much explaining. So little time.

Apollo shrugs. "It's inevitable I will see him again. You and I are forever. I know I can't separate you from your family. I've accepted I will need to interact with them on occasion."

My jaw drops. I pick it back up to make words. "You and I are not forever. We are never."

"I disagree," Apollo says in the tone of a man stating his opinion on where to go for dinner.

"You don't get to decide what I do with my life. You can't just declare that I am yours for eternity."

Apollo lifts his arm, holds out the small water bottle to me. "I am offering. Again. I have offered you myself, immortality, the life of a goddess. I am tired of you turning me down."

Nectar.

"You can't make me drink that."

He smiles. The predator is back. One step toward me. "I could. I've already shown you how irresistible I can be. I got you to sleep in my arms last night, didn't I?"

I shake my head, shift my feet, refuse to give ground. "That's not fair."

I chose to sleep there; he didn't make me. At least it felt like my choice.

"I wasn't even really trying last night. Imagine if I put all of my effort into making you mine."

"Would you really want me against my will? Wouldn't that defeat the purpose of all this effort? You wouldn't actually be winning me."

"Maybe I've decided that force is acceptable. For now. I can always woo you tomorrow. Or the day after. I'll have all the time in the world to win you."

I shift my bow. My fingers itch to draw an arrow and shoot Apollo. But the arrow I need is on the other side of the yard, buried in his ridiculous love letter.

I look directly at Apollo. I don't dare let my eyes wander to the arrow that is massive in my mind. He can't know what I am after.

I take a few steps toward him, following the path the arrow traveled. I want Apollo to think I am coming to him, to drink the nectar, and take his gift.

A smile blossoms on his face.

I stop in the middle of the yard. He beams. Holds out his immortal gift.

I stand, immobile. I won't take the few steps to reach him, drink the nectar. I can't turn away and run to the arrow I need. I can't even look at it. I am stuck. Stranded. In the middle of my own back yard.

"Kass? What are you doing?" My eyes fly to Nik where he stands in the sliding glass door, the kitchen behind him.

He is wearing a white T-shirt.

The blood drains out of me, pours into the earth below me.

Apollo soaks it up, blushes, his lips twisting into a smile as he turns. "Nikolas."

Nik steps onto the patio and stares at the man, the god, before him. "Apollo?"

I take advantage of the distraction Nik accidentally provides. Apollo does not have his bow drawn; Nik is safe. For the moment. I need to be fast, shift Apollo's attention away from Nik as soon as I can. I just need a moment out of his sight, a moment to retrieve Zeus's gift. I move quickly, try not to disturb the air around me as I reach the arrow and pull it free.

My eyes lock on Apollo's back as I nock the arrow and click it into the release. I draw and sight Apollo, focusing on the outline of his shoulder blades under his shirt.

As if he had been watching me all along, Apollo turns and raises his bow in one smooth motion. The golden tip of his arrow points at me. The only thing in the world is that tip focused on me.

Fear and peace battle in me. I am terrified of the arrow pointed at me, delighted it is not pointed at Nik. My breath is quick and shallow. My chest and shoulders flutter with the movement of the tiny bursts of air.

I push my gaze from the golden arrow up to Apollo. He stares back at me. I know he doesn't have to be looking at me to kill me.

Apollo's arms are steady. Mine are not.

My bow quivers.

Apollo sees the tremor and smirks. "You know the fundamental difference between you and I, Kassandra?"

I don't answer. Too many answers come to mind to choose just one.

"I shoot to kill," Apollo answers for me. This was not an answer I had considered. "I am a hunter. You shoot at targets. You have never caused a death. I don't think you can do it now."

The words sink into me. This is the true answer. The one that matters. I am not a hunter, a killer. Even though I did cause Manuel Striker's death. The tremor in my arms grows. My bow bounces in the air.

"Plus, you love me," Apollo adds.

My mind flips through images of things I love. Apollo does not appear. The last image is Nik. My brother. My other half. The person I will save.

I lock my eyes on Apollo's. The bow steadies.

Apollo shakes his head. A faint smiles ghosts across his face as his finger shifts on the string of his bow.

I breathe in, let the breath out, shift my jaw, press the release.

The arrow sails toward Apollo. The green-striped arrow skims past him, a hair away from his ear.

He does not flinch.

I see my shot was off in the same second I see I fired too late.

Apollo's arrow is in the air.

Nik is moving.

Nik and the golden arrow collide in front of me.

My vision replays in front of me. This time I can see it all.

The arrow hits Nik, sinks into his flesh. His blood begins to run. Nik gasps, tries to pull air into his injured lung.

I drop the useless bow, run to Nik, and fall to my knees. My hand flies to Nik's chest. I try to hold in the flood of red that leaks around the arrow, stains his white shirt.

"What have I done?" a shattered voice cries.

It is not mine.

I look up. Apollo stands at my side. His facade is cracked. Anguish mars his pale face. His bow dangles from limp fingers at his side. He looks down at Nik, at the arrow that sticks up into the air, bobs with Nik's efforts to breathe.

"You did exactly what I told you you would do." My voice is strong. It bites through the tears that course down my cheeks. "I couldn't stop it." My voice slips to a whisper. "I never could have stopped it. Fate always wins."

Chapter Twenty-Seven

"I can heal him." Apollo drops to his knees beside Nik, stretches out his hands. He rips the blood-red shirt free, exposing the wound. Apollo stops, his hands hovering over Nik's bare skin.

"No. I can't." His words are shredded.

"Why? You healed me! All you have to do is touch him." I reach over, pushing his hands down.

"It won't work, Kassandra." Apollo lifts his eyes to mine. I watch them flood. "I intended for that arrow to kill. That's what it will do. I can't take it back. I can't heal him."

Apollo's words sink into me. He meant for that arrow to kill me. Me. But Nik stepped in the way. He caught Apollo's intent. This is what Zeus meant.

My own arrow, tipped by Zeus's gift. I meant to kill Apollo in that moment, would have done anything to keep Nik safe. I would have killed Apollo. I would have watched him die in Nik's arms.

Not only did I fail to stop fate, this time I caused it. My intention to kill Apollo is why Nik has a golden arrow sticking out of his chest.

"I'm sorry," I whisper. To Nik. To Apollo. To myself.

My eyes drift from Apollo. I want to look at Nik, want to be with him through the end. I can't make myself look at the blood. My eyes travel, bounce around the yard, anywhere but at my failure.

My bow, discarded in the grass.

The arrow, tipped by Zeus, stuck into a palm on the far side of my yard.

Apollo's water bottle nestled in the grass where Apollo stood before drawing his bow.

"Nectar." I zoom back to Apollo.

He shakes his head once. He has no time for me; he is with Nik.

"Apollo."

My intent catches him, forces him to look at me.

"Nectar. If Nik drinks it, he'll be healed." This will work. It has too. It might not.

Apollo's gaze leaves me again, travels inward. He gives one short nod and then is across the yard, the discarded water bottle in his hand. He returns and hands it to me. "It might work."

"Might? It will make him immortal. Keep him from dying."

A huge gasp from Nik pulls us from the nectar to the dying boy on the ground.

"I don't know if nectar has ever been given to anyone who was already dying. I'm not certain it will work." Apollo kneels on the other side of Nik, pulls his torso onto his lap, raising Nik into an almost sitting position.

I don't know if this is a good idea. But it is the only one I have, my last chance to save my brother, undo what I have done. I uncap the bottle and lift it to Nik's lips. He looks back at me, confusion and pain swirling on his face.

I will have a lot of explaining to do if this works.

Nik sips.

I tip the bottle, force him to chug the entire contents.

"Now what?" I ask Apollo. I push back my hair. A warm smear of blood moves from my hand to my face.

"We wait. He lives. Or he does not."

I pull out my phone, ready to call an ambulance, ask for mortal medicine to assist the magic of the gods.

Apollo puts his hand over mine. "We wait," he repeats. "Your hospital cannot help him, not any more than I could. Listen to his breath."

I silence. Air whistles softly, a gnarled pull through Nik's open mouth. The sound dims as the breaths slow.

"Is he getting better or worse?" I ask. I hear the panic edge into my voice. I can't tuck it back.

Apollo looks down at Nik. "I don't know."

We watch the arrow bob with each small breath.

"He can't heal if the arrow is still in him." The words are soft. I'm not sure who speaks them. I don't have time to process, decide who uttered them, before Apollo's hands wrap around the arrow's shaft and pull.

The arrow slips free of Nik's skin. A fresh gush of blood pours out of him, soaking Apollo's jeans.

"What did you do?" Now I know the words were not mine. This was Apollo's idea. My hand flies to Nik's chest, trying to push the blood back in.

For a moment, it seems I succeed. The flow of blood slows to a trickle, then stops. I pull my hand away, look at the still gaping wound. The flesh knits back together, from the inside out, until only a faint scratch remains.

"Oh, my god," I whisper.

"Yes?" Apollo replies.

I look up to see a full smile dancing across his face.

"It worked."

"Yes," Apollo replies.

"He's immortal."

"Yes."

***

"What have I done?" I think I ask myself.

Apollo doesn't answer. That doesn't mean the words were only in my head.

I look to Nik for an answer. I expect to see him looking up at me, questions of his own lacing his gaze. Instead, he is asleep. His chest moves smoothly up and down with the easy movement of air. He is peaceful, calm, an angel sleeping soundly in the arms of his god.

He isn't my brother anymore. He belongs to Apollo.

I stand and stumble toward the house.

"Kassandra?" Apollo calls after me.

I ignore him, let my feet carry me through the doors to the kitchen and up the stairs to my bathroom. A stranger stands in the mirror. A girl warrior defeated in battle. Her hair is a tangled mess, half up, half twined around itself. A nest of snakes. Blood streaks her face, smears her clothes. Tears cut rivulets of clean down her cheeks and neck.

I don't remember crying. I wish I had felt that release.

I peel off my clothes and step into the shower. I run the water boiling hot. I want to scorch away the day, the last few weeks. I want to go back to being a girl who has a brother.

I close my eyes, let the hot spray pound onto my face.

I do not think about my back yard.

I think of nothing.

I stand until the water runs cold, then embrace the cold bite for a moment before turning off the water. Clean and pink, I slip on sweats and a T-shirt. The mess of clothes on the bathroom floor is wadded into a ball for transport downstairs to bury in a garbage can.

The living room stops me at the bottom of the stairs. Apollo is on the couch. Nik's head rests on his lap. They are both clean, bloodless. At least on the outside. I don't know about the inside. Do immortals have blood? Nik has on a fresh white shirt.

I expected them to be gone, already perched in Olympus, not waiting to taunt me.

I turn away and move into the kitchen, back out through the glass doors. It's time to survey the carnage. I look to the middle of the yard, the spot where Nik caught the arrow meant for me, fell, spilled his blood on the grass. There is no blood stain. The notes are gone from the target, the scattered arrows tucked away somewhere. My bow does not lie where I know I dropped it.

Nothing happened here.

I move around the corner of the house, open the garbage can and lift out a bag of trash, tuck the soiled ball underneath. I replace the lid. Done. Everything cleaned up.

It is over.

I break.

Huge, gasping sobs tear up from my chest, spilling out into the air. I saved Nik. He is alive. He is not my brother anymore. He is immortal. He belongs to the gods. Apollo will take him away, settle him into the mansion on Olympus where he can watch me on the big screen. I will never see him again.

I am alone. No one comes to comfort me, find out why I am crying.

Nik will never tease away my tears again.

I pull myself together, bring the tears to a shuddering stop. He is alive. That is what really matters. The only thing left for me to do is say goodbye. Apollo might take his prize away at any moment.

I turn, needing goodbye.

Soft singing drifts from the living room. It draws me. Apollo runs his fingers through Nik's hair as he sings a lullaby of sorts. Apollo's voice is just as beautiful as the man. I stand in the doorway, watch, listen. There is an entire choir in his voice. They sing in a language I can't understand, but the sound soothes me anyway. Like listening to the ocean caress the shore.

I wish I were in Apollo's place. Nik's head on my leg. My fingers touching his hair, his skin. His warmth reminds me he is alive.

I wish I were in Nik's place. Curled into Apollo's warmth. His skin against my own. Absorbing the song he sings for me.

I am jealous of them both. I want to be both, have them both.

I can have neither.

Apollo's voice trails off under the weight of my gaze.

"Why is he still sleeping?" I ask. I move into the room and perch on the arm of a chair. I am afraid to get too close. It will only make me want them more. Miss them more.

"He's changing. This always happens when a mortal drinks nectar."

"Oh." Nik looks different already. Stronger. More polished. Radiant and perfect. Like a god. I bite my lip and close my eyes. Looking at him now is almost as bad as watching him die.

"You saved him."

I shake my head. "No. You did. It was your nectar."

"I didn't think to have him drink it. That was your idea. He would have died without it."

"Maybe that would have been better," I whisper.

"What?" Apollo's words bite me. "Why would you say that?"

"He would be dead. But he would still be my brother. I could mourn him, let him go." I scrub at my eyes, push away the tears that itch there. "Instead, you are going to take him from me. You already have."

"He is still your brother."

"No. He's your immortal. He has become what you wanted me to be. An eternal plaything to be tucked away on Olympus."

"I have no intention of taking him."

"What?"

"Was my letter to you unclear? I wanted you to drink the nectar, not Nik. While I do love Nik, I don't love him the right way. I know myself. I would grow bored, toss him aside. I guess I already have."

"And you wouldn't do the same with me?"

"No. You wouldn't let me. I would have to convince you every day to love me. It would keep me on my toes, keep my love honest."

I can't imagine battling Apollo every day, fighting to exert whatever will I can muster in the face of his persuasion. It is beautifully terrifying.

"What now?" I ask. This is not a safe subject. "What happens to Nik?"

"He lives forever."

"With you."

"Kassandra. Listen to me. I'm not taking Nik away from you."

"I'm not going to Olympus with you two. I wasn't willing to go with you alone. I'm certainly not interested in being your third wheel."

Apollo sighs. It churns the air in the room. "Shut up and listen. To the words I am saying, not the words you expect."

I choke on the urge to talk, to argue.

"Nik is staying here." Apollo holds up a hand when I open my mouth again. "With you. And your parents. He is not going to Olympus with me. Neither are you."

I want to believe him. Believe I will still have my brother at the end of this day.

"Nik can stay here," Apollo continues. "At least for now. It will likely be a long time before anyone notices he's truly different. He is a teenager, they are constantly shifting, changing. He can remain your brother until he decides it is time to move on."

"That seems too good to be true. What's the catch? Do I have to have sex with you? Promise to be your immortal bride?"

Apollo laughs at me. This is our default state. Me angry. Frustrated. Apollo amused at my distress. Maybe it will all be okay.

"He just has to drink the nectar. Every day."

"If he doesn't?"

"If he stops, the days that have passed will fall upon him all at once, the damage of time inflicted in a single moment. His body will not have time to deal with the damage. It will kill him."

"That's it. He lives on earth, immortal, until he decides to leave. All he has to do is drink nectar."

Apollo's eyebrow nods.

"I feel like there should be a catch." There is always a catch with this god-man.

Apollo shakes his head. "I feel guilty. I should have believed you. I can't make myself charge you for this gift."

"Thank you so much for your generosity."

Apollo's face falls. My sarcasm boomerangs back to smack me. Maybe Apollo is doing the best he can. This is how he thinks the world works. It *is* how the world works, for him.

"That's how gifts are supposed to be, you know," I try in a gentler voice. It is nicer for us both. "They aren't supposed to have strings attached."

The smile that creeps across Apollo's face makes him look like an innocent, a little boy. I can't hold back my answering smile.

This feels right. He isn't pushing me for something I don't want to give. We are almost equal in our power.

I take a deep breath, a surge of an idea pushing me. "Can I ask you something?"

Apollo nods.

"It's a huge favor, really. I thought of something you could do. Something that might help me. Maybe you. Maybe Nik."

"What is it, Kassandra?"

"I know you can't take away my visions, or the curse you added."

Apollo flinches.

"But you could give someone else a gift, or maybe it's a curse. I'm still not sure. Something that could interact with my gift, my curse."

"I don't know what you mean."

I can't blame him. The words are jumbled in my head, the idea so unlikely to work, that I am surprised I manage to get out any words at all.

I try again. "Nik. You could give him a gift. A something." I stand and move to the couch, into their world, settle on the cushion at Nik's waist. I rest my hand on his cheek, my eyes on Nik's dark lashes, avoiding looking at Apollo.

"You could make him share my visions."

"You would wish that on him?"

"Like I said, I'm not sure if it's a gift or a curse." I lift my eyes to Apollo. "But if he sees what I see, he can help me change things. People will believe him." I pause.

"I won't be alone."

Apollo's hand covers mine. His eyes cover mine.

"Are you sure? You know I can't take it back once it is given."

I'm not sure. Not at all. I don't know if this is a gift Nik will welcome, or even one he can handle. His whole world is about to change as it is. This might be one thing too many. But I need him to have it. I need him on my side. My other half.

I won't survive another failed attempt to change fate, to save someone I love. It will push me into insanity.

My eyes say yes to Apollo's eyes.

Apollo lifts my hand from Nik's face.

Motion twitches in the doorway, catches my attention. I turn.

A snake slithers into the room, it's tongue aflicker.

I scream.

My legs up on the couch, I back over Nik's legs to curl into the corner of the couch. It is not far enough from the snake. I need to be somewhere, anywhere, else.

The snake twines up the leg of the couch next to Apollo. Apollo holds out a hand, welcomes the snake.

I am ice. I watch.

The snake slinks over Nik's shoulder. The story Mom tells every year replays in my mind, this time with images right in front of me. The snake curls onto Nik's chest, stretches, reaches, until its head is next to Nik's ear.

The flickering tongue touches Nik's ear once, twice. The snake pulls away, turns toward me, slithers in my direction. A loaded stare.

I must win the short staring contest. Not due to strength. I am just too terrified to blink, to let the snake out of my sight. The snake shifts, moves to the floor and back to the kitchen.

I am still frozen in the corner of the couch.

Apollo reaches for me, brushes his fingers across my face. It melts me, brings me back to life.

"I hope this works out for you, Kassandra." Apollo lifts Nik's head from his lap and stands, settles Nik onto the couch cushion. "It's time for me to go."

"Wait. What about Nik?" I scoot toward Apollo, toward the edge of the couch, but don't put my feet on the floor. There could be anything under the couch. Monsters. More snakes.

"Is Nik okay?"

Apollo smiles and takes my hand. "He will wake. He will be confused. You will have to explain what has happened. How he has changed."

He leans close, rests his lips gently on my cheek. I want to keep them there forever.

"I'll be watching. When Nik is ready, I will come." Apollo straightens, my hand still held in his. For a moment more, we are connected.

"When you are ready, I will come." He squeezes my hand, then turns and moves to the front door.

Framed by the bright sunlight outside, he looks at Nik and I one last time. Then he is gone.

I sit with my brother until he wakes, then I begin the long story. I invite him to conquer fate with me.

About the Author

S usan Monroe McGrath is a teacher by day and a writer by night. She lives with her herd of humans and cats in Colorado. She posts short fiction, book reviews and whatever other bookish things strike her fancy at https://susanmonroemcgrath.home.blog/ Join her newsletter at susanmonroemcgrath.substack.com/

Books and Stories by this Author

Short Stories

The Passenger

Grace picks up an ordinary passenger in her cab. The message he leaves behind, however, is anything but ordinary.

The Vacant Kiss

A single kiss sparks new life in a woman, but may not mean what she wishes it did.

Pub Crawlers

Three people Brione hoped to never see again walk into her bar, forcing her to finally react to the last time they were together.

Fog Bound

Gwen takes her normal morning walk, but something comes with her out of the fog.

I Remember Everything

Annabeth remembers everything about her relationship with George. Plus some things that never happened.

Solitaire

A woman working alone in the wilds of Utah finds she might be less alone than she thought.

Under Glass

A cross country drive with someone that isn't quite a friend leads to an unexpected roadside attraction.

Figments

This collection of short stories, flash fiction, and drabbles spans over a decade of writing. Most of the pieces contain a speculative element. All of them are figments of my imagination.

Scarlet Sky

Three girls head out on an overnight adventure, intending to leave their mark before their friendship is broken apart. A slip, a storm, and a shove derail their plans, leaving a legacy behind.

Roswell

A woman waits for her long estranged best friend next to the alien welcome sign in Roswell. She hopes for reconciliation, but instead finds the source of their estrangement is not what it seemed.

You Can Always Find a Friend at the Mall

A trip to the mall to drop off a box of clothes for donation takes a turn when Trix stops to get her fortune from an antique toy fortune teller. Disregarding the fortune may lead to her demise.

Young Adult Novels

Variations on a Tango Girl

Mavis transfers to a school of the arts at the start of her junior year to boost her dance credits and make herself a more well-rounded and attractive applicant. She doesn't plan on landing the lead in Chicago. She doesn't plan on meeting a dark and dreamy boy.

Challenged by Notre Dame to write a personal essay describing how she is incomplete, Mavis first thinks of her absent mother. Mavis is pushed by her best friend Fletch to go deeper, but can't see past the hole her mother left behind.

Mavis must balance the mounting pressures of school, rehearsals, and developing relationships while learning to see herself as more than the Mavis her mom left behind. On the line are her essay, her future, and her heart.

Sighted

Kassandra was kissed by a snake. Now she is kissing Apollo.

The first kiss happened when she was only two. The flick of a forked tongue gave her the gift of foresight. The sink of fangs into her flesh took her arm away. Kassandra doesn't mourn the loss of her arm and it hasn't stopped her from becoming a competitive archer. The gift of foresight has allowed her to save the lives of friends and strangers.

Now Kassandra is seventeen and Apollo is back. He wants compensation for the snake's gift- a gift he sent. He wants Kassandra. Kassandra is not interested in being a god's eternal companion, but she does agree to a single kiss.

Kissing a god is divine, but it comes with a curse. Kassandra can still see the future, but she is now powerless to change it. Her words and manipulation that have worked so well to alter fate fail her.

Apollo twines his way into Kassandra's mortal Florida life, crashing into her classes, charming her parents and her twin brother Nikolas. Apollo still wants his prize. Kassandra just wants her normal back.

When Kassandra has a vision of Nikolas pierced by an arrow from Apollo's bow, no one believes her. She cannot convince Apollo that he would ever hurt Nikolas. She cannot convince Apollo that he has cursed himself.

Words will not save her brother. Kassandra will have to use her bow.

*9 7 9 8 9 9 3 5 3 8 3 2 7 *